L'il T will do anything for a dog.

"You'd really do that?" Granpa T says. He's shaking the beer can. It's empty. "You'd sell that Game Boy?"

I take a deep breath. "I already did it." I reach in my pocket and I pull out money. A lot of money.

"Today," I say, "in school."

We're sitting there looking at my hand all stuffed full of money.

"I want a dog," I say. "I want that dog."

Granpa T stands up. Way up high in the trees, the frogs are screaming. Across the street, the lady's air conditioner comes roaring on.

"I plan on naming him Buddy," I say, "because that's what he'll be, my buddy."

I shove the money back in my pocket. I look up and there's Granpa T looking down at me in the dark evening. Behind him is the big old sky all full of stars. I cross my fingers.

"I'll go talk to your daddy," Granpa T says, and eases on inside.

OTHER BOOKS YOU MAY ENJOY

Almost Home	Joan Bauer
The Call of the Wild	Jack London
Ghost Dog Secrets	Peg Kehret
The Great Wide Sea	M. H. Herlong
Jefferson's Sons	Kimberly Brubaker Bradley
One for the Murphys	Linda Mullaly Hunt
Saint Louis Armstrong Beach	Brenda Woods
Secret Saturdays	Torrey Maldonado
Three Times Lucky	Sheila Turnage

BUDDY

M. H. Herlong

PUFFIN BOOKS
An Imprint of Penguin Group (USA) Inc.

PUFFIN BOOKS
An imprint of Penguin Young Readers Group
Published by the Penguin Group
Penguin Group (USA) Inc.
375 Hudson Street
New York, New York 10014, U.S.A.

USA / Canada / UK / Ireland / Australia / New Zealand / India / South Africa / China
Penguin Books Ltd, Registered Offices: 80 Strand, London WC2R 0RL, England

For more information about the Penguin Group visit www.penguin.com

First published in the United States of America by Viking,
a division of Penguin Young Readers Group, 2012
Published by Puffin Books, an imprint of Penguin Young Readers Group, 2013

THE LIBRARY OF CONGRESS HAS CATALOGED THE VIKING EDITION AS FOLLOWS:
Herlong, M. H.
Buddy / by M. H. Herlong
p. cm.
Summary: Twelve-year-old Li'l T and his family face great losses caused by Hurricane Katrina, including leaving Buddy, their very special, three-legged dog, behind when they must evacuate.
ISBN 978-0-670-01403-3 (hardcover)
[1. Family life—Louisiana—Fiction. 2. Dogs—Fiction. 3. Hurricane Katrina, 2005—Fiction.
4. African Americans—Fiction. 5. Lost and found possessions—Fiction.
6. New Orleans (La.)—Fiction.]
1. Title. PZ7.H431267Bud 2012
[Fic]—dc23
2011042854

Puffin Books ISBN 978-0-14-242544-2

Printed in the United States of America

9 10

To New Orleans

1

We found Buddy in the middle of St. Roch Avenue at 8:45 on a Sunday morning. That's the way Granpa T would start this story. "It was early April," he'd say. "The spring of 2005."

"Is that so?" somebody else would say.

"It's a fact," Granpa T would say, and then he'd nod his head. "I'm going to tell you a story about a dog—a three-legged dog—and a little black boy with no more sense than God gave a grasshopper."

But Granpa T ain't telling this story. I'm telling it. My name is Tyrone Elijah Roberts, just like my daddy and Granpa T before him. Everybody calls Daddy "T Junior." Everybody calls me "Li'l T."

So this story starts up in the car. We're on our way to church. It's hot in the car and we're crowded. Daddy's driving and Mama's sitting in the front seat fanning herself. I'm squeezed in between them and looking at my Game Boy.

I'm about to make it to the next level.

My little sister's in the back playing the fool with the baby. She's shaking these big old plastic keys in front of his face and saying, "Grab them. Come on, Baby Terrell. You can do it."

And Granpa T's sitting beside the baby seat, leaning back with his mouth open like he's sleeping but he ain't sleeping. He's just gone someplace he goes when he don't like where he is.

"We need a bigger car, T Junior," Mama says.

Daddy don't say nothing.

"Li'l T's almost thirteen years old. Pretty soon, his feet are going to be sticking out the front window."

Daddy still don't say nothing.

"And when Tanya and Terrell both get bigger, it's going to be *way* too crowded in this old car."

"I already said," Daddy starts up, "we'll go looking when I get that increase at work. It don't help to bring it up now."

Mama casts her eye at Daddy. Then she sighs. "It's just so hot," she says. "And it's only April."

Daddy nods, and I miss my shot, and it's Game Over.

We're riding by the Tomato Man. It's too early for good

tomatoes, but he's out there selling other stuff just like he does every Sunday morning.

"What's he got for sale today?" Mama says.

Daddy leans forward a little bit and says, "Sign says collard greens."

"I don't want any collard greens," Mama says.

And then all a sudden Daddy slams on the brakes, and Mama screams, and I'm bending forward toward the dashboard. Mama's arm slams into my chest, and those plastic keys come flying over the seat and smack the back of my head, and the baby starts crying, and Granpa T sits up straight and says something I can't write down in this story.

Then the whole world's still.

We're sitting in the hot car and the baby's crying and Mama finally says, "What was that, T Junior?"

And Daddy says, "I think I hit a dog."

•◆•

Daddy climbs out of the car first. He opens the door and it creaks like it's going to fall off but it don't. He looks up toward the front of the car.

"Oh, Lord," he says, and I'm crawling out his door while Mama's grabbing at my leg saying, "Wait," but one thing I ain't doing is waiting.

It's a black dog. A black dog with long, straight fur. He's laying flat on the street. His tail is stretched out behind him, and he's still as a stone.

I kneel down in the street right beside him.

"Be careful," Daddy says, but he don't stop me.

"Hey, boy," I say. I reach out my hand toward the dog real slow and touch his head just a little bit. "Easy, now. Easy," I say.

The dog twitches. And then all a sudden he lifts up his head and looks straight at me.

"He's alive," Daddy shouts, and everybody starts piling out the car to come see.

That dog don't take his eyes off me. He's looking at me like he's wondering who I am, and I'm looking right back. His eyes are soft and big and dark, dark brown, with black going all around the rims. He's got a sprinkling of white fur across his forehead and down the top of his nose, sort of in the shape of a heart.

Everybody's crowding around, but me and that dog are still looking at each other. He's got a long, thin scar over one of his eyes. The fur around the scar goes every which way, making him look like he's got a buck moth caterpillar stuck on his forehead. Under his chin and down his throat, the fur is mostly white. One front paw is supposed to be white, too, but it's so dirty it looks almost brown.

"He sure is dirty," Mama says. She's standing there with her hands on her hips and Tanya's hanging on her like she might fly away.

Granpa T bends down and looks at the dog and says, "His hind leg's broke."

"How do you know that?" Daddy says.

"I use my eyes," Granpa T says, and points.

And sure enough, anybody can see. The top back leg is kind of covering it up, but once you look, you can see the other back leg is bent the wrong way and there's something white sticking out through the fur. That dog's leg ain't just broke. It's broke bad.

I'm rubbing the dog's head now. He's started panting like nobody's business laying there on the hard street in the hot sun where the shadow from the oak trees ain't even close to him.

I can feel the hard bone under his soft fur and the way his skin moves a little when I push my hand over the round top of his head. His eyes stretch open and I curl my fingers into the thick fur on his neck.

I bend down and touch the top of the dog's head with my

nose. He smells like dog sweat and old, wet leaves and dry dust all at the same time.

"Be careful, Li'l T," Mama says.

"Ain't nothing to worry about," Granpa T says. "That's one gentle dog."

"You can't tell that," Daddy says. "He's still half knocked out."

Granpa T just shrugs his shoulders.

"What's your name?" I whisper to the dog.

He sticks up his tongue and licks my chin. I must taste good because he does it twice. Then he shifts a little and his broke leg moves and he yelps and starts to wiggle like he wants to get up.

"Easy, boy," I say again. "Easy."

And he settles right down and lays still.

"What are we going to do, Daddy?" I say.

Daddy's standing there wiping his face with a tissue. Granpa T's leaning on the side of the car with his arms crossed over his chest.

Mama looks over at the Tomato Man down the road. "Who's dog is this?" she yells.

Tomato Man's standing up under his umbrella. He's looking at us like we're a movie show. "Ain't nobody's," he hollers back. "Just a street dog."

"But who feeds him?" Mama yells.

Tomato Man shrugs up his shoulders.

Mama looks down at the dog. "Doesn't look like anybody feeds him," she says.

The baby's crying in the car. Tanya's twisting her feet in her sandal shoes and wrinkling up Mama's dress in her hand.

Mama looks at her watch and says, "We're going to be late for church."

"He needs a doctor," Granpa T says.

"We can't pay a doctor for no dog," Daddy says.

"But somebody's got to help him," Granpa T says.

"Well, we can't take him with us," Mama says. "There's not enough room in the car."

"We can't just leave him here neither," Daddy says.

I'm still kneeling down by the dog. Now he's resting his head in the palm of my hand, and I'm thinking that my hand is going to smell just like dog.

Just like this dog.

I look up at all those people fussing and I don't even think about it. All a sudden, I just blurt it out.

"There'll be plenty enough room," I say, "if I walk."

Every one of them stops talking. They all look down and stare at me.

"Put the dog in the back," I say. "Tanya can take my seat. Somebody at church will know what to do."

"You're going to walk to church?" Daddy says.

"He's not old enough to do that," Mama says. "This neighborhood—"

"How old are you, boy?" Granpa T says.

"Thirteen next October," I say.

"I was picking cotton when I was your age," Granpa T says. He turns to Mama. "I think he can walk five blocks to church. T Junior, put that dog in the car. Standing in this heat ain't good for my heart."

When Granpa T says what to do, everybody does it. Mama's mouth is all screwed up like she's sucking a lemon, but she don't say nothing. She buckles Tanya into the front seat and sticks a pacifier in the baby's mouth so he stops crying.

"Okay, dog," Daddy says. "I'm going to pick you up and you ain't going to bite me. We got a deal?"

That dog's looking at Daddy like he ain't too sure about this deal.

Daddy squats down and slowly starts to work his arms up under the dog. Granpa T's helping with the broke leg. The dog twists his head back and forth like he's trying to look at both of them at the same time. When Daddy lifts him up off the ground, the dog makes a noise like a squeaky toy and then a yelpy sound.

Daddy makes a sound, too, like *umph*. "He's boney," Daddy says, "but he's heavy enough."

That dog is whimpering and wiggling like he wants to get away but then Daddy hustles him into the car. The dog takes up all of Tanya's seat and more, his front feet passing up under the baby seat and his head almost laying in the baby's lap.

That dog is looking at Baby Terrell but I can't stop looking at the dog. At first I think his big old eyes are sad and scared because he's hurt and maybe because he's hungry. Next I think they're glad and happy because he's out of the sun and maybe because he thinks we're going to feed him. Then he settles his head down and turns his eyes on Mama.

"You watch that dog with my baby, Granpa T," Mama says. "If he takes even a little nip I'll throw him out on the street, broke leg and all."

"He ain't going to bite Baby Terrell," I say. "Just look at his eyes."

Mama gives me a look. "You don't know anything about that dog," she says.

"I know that much," I say.

"Hmph," Mama says.

Then they're all in the car and the doors slam shut. Daddy

leans out the window. “Keep on walking down this street, son, until you get to St. Claude. Turn left and go on until you see the church. We’ll be inside looking for you.”

I nod. They drive off.

“What are you going to call that dog?” Tomato Man hollers.

“What makes you think I’m going to call him anything?”

Tomato Man laughs and picks up his newspaper. “I know what I know,” is all he says.

2

I started up wanting a dog the day after I was born. At least, that's what I always tell people. We were living in a double, and my best friend Jamilla and her aunt were living on the other side. For extra money, Mama was making pralines to sell out of the house and watching Jamilla while Jamilla's aunt was at work. We played on the front porch every day, and I remember every single dog that ever walked by. And there were a lot.

When I was about five or six, a boy down the street named Melvin had a yellow dog that chased a ball. Every day when Jamilla and me got home from school, we watched him walk out with that dog and head to the park. We asked if we could come but he said we were too little. I told Jamilla I wanted a dog just like that. She drew me one on a piece of paper and said, “Here.” Mama stuck it up on my wall and said, “That dog almost looks alive.” I was thinking it was a good picture but it wasn’t *that* good.

When I was seven years old, I told my daddy I wanted a dog.

Mama was walking round with a great big stomach, and Daddy said, “We can’t have a dog. We’re going to have a baby.”

I said, “I want a dog, not a baby.”

Daddy said, “You don’t get to choose.”

When I was nine years old, I told my daddy I still wanted a dog, and he said, “We got a toddler baby now. We ain’t got room for a dog.”

When I was ten years old, we moved down the street to live with Granpa T. He said he had a big old empty house and couldn’t work anymore because of his heart trouble, and what were we doing paying rent anyway. Mama had started cooking up lunches to sell, too, so she could use a bigger kitchen. And to tell the truth, Granpa T wasn’t as strong as he ought to be. Jamilla’s drawing got all ripped up when we took it off the wall. She said she would do another one, but I said, “Don’t worry about it. We got a yard now—even though there ain’t hardly no grass.”

So I told my daddy we had enough room now and I still wanted a dog. But he said times were hard and he didn't have the money to feed a dog.

When Mama's stomach got big again, I knew there wasn't no point saying I wanted a dog. We were going to have another baby, and there wasn't no more money than there was before.

And since Christmas, there ain't even been as much. Jamilla and her aunt just up and moved. One day when the aunt came by after work to get Jamilla, Mama started up showing off the little plastic bags she had just bought to put her pralines in. Each bag was just big enough for one praline and each one said *Mama's pralines* in this pinky-red color Mama took about two hours to pick out. She had just bought boxes and boxes of them plus two rolls of ribbon to tie them shut. The aunt was standing there nodding and saying how nice that was going to look. Then all a sudden she stopped nodding and she said, "I need to tell y'all something. We're moving to Chicago. I got a better job. It'll be a better school. We're leaving this weekend."

We were just standing there staring at her and then she said, "Y'all have been good to Jamilla for ten years, and you're like family. But we have to go." Just before Jamilla walked out the door, she turned around and waved. "I'll write you a letter, Li'l T," she said, "and then you can write me back." And that's the last time I ever talked to her.

So then there was nobody to ride the bus with and nobody to do my homework with and nobody to keep Tanya off when I wanted to play my Game Boy. Mama had spent all her money on those little plastic bags and she didn't have anybody extra to babysit, just Tanya and Terrell, and you don't get money for babysitting your own children. I knew there wasn't no way in the world they were ever going to let me have a dog of my own. Then Melvin's yellow dog from down the street ran off, and I didn't even have somebody else's dog to look at anymore. I went in my room and laid down on my bed and didn't move for about a week. I just stared at the ceiling and thought that I should have let Jamilla draw me one more picture because then at least I'd have that instead of nothing at all.

So now I'm walking on past the Tomato Man down the street toward the church. I'm thinking about how it's been over three months and Jamilla still ain't wrote me a letter. I'm getting sweaty in my Sunday clothes and my shoes are getting dusty.

And then I start thinking about how that dog put his nose in the palm of my hand. I start thinking about his big old eyes looking up at me. I start thinking about his broke leg and the way his ribs were sticking up when he was laying on his side. I hold my hand up to my face and I smell his smell all over again. Dog sweat, dry dust, and old, wet leaves.

Then I remember how the preacher always says nobody knows what God's plan might be, so I decide right then and there I'd better make a plan of my own.

I look up at the sky—just once—and then I get busy.

•◆•

I walk in at the church when they're singing. They're singing loud and they're swaying. The choir starts clapping their hands and everybody joins in. I walk down the aisle to where my family's standing. They're singing with the rest of them. When they see me, Granpa T leans over to Mama and says, "Told you," but she don't look too happy about it.

I squeeze in beside Daddy, and Tanya leans around and looks up at me and smiles real big. That girl sure is all teeth when she grins.

When the song is done, we all sit down and the preacher starts talking about the meetings and committees and who's supposed to do what, but I'm thinking about the dog and wondering where he is. I poke Daddy and whisper in his ear. Daddy points and then I see him. He's laying up against the wall at the end of the aisle. Somebody's put a bowl of water by him but now his head is down and he looks like he's asleep. I start to get up, but Daddy puts his hand on my arm and makes me stay put.

While I'm looking at that dog, he lifts up his head and sees me. I swear I see his tail go *thump*.

Then we come to the time when the preacher asks us to share our problems. Mrs. Washington is still worried about her nephew in Iraq and we all pray for him. Mr. Boudreaux says his daddy is down in his back. He can't work, and all he does now is sit in his dark room watching TV and saying nobody needs him anymore. So we all pray for Mr. Boudreaux's daddy. One little girl stands up and says she's worried about her cat because it ain't come home in three days. We pray for the cat.

Then I poke Daddy. He points to Granpa T who's already standing up. Granpa T says he's got a story to tell but he don't know how it ends. He says that's where he needs the help. He says we're driving in the car to church this morning and the family is all squeezed in because the car's too small and we can't buy another one. We ain't got the money.

And the people say, "Uh-huh," or "I know all about that!"

"Then," Granpa T says, "we hit a dog—*wham*!" And he claps his hands together so loud Tanya jumps.

The people suck in their breath and say, "Mercy!"

Granpa T's standing there looking at his feet and shaking his head. He says this story would be over if that dog had died, but that dog didn't die.

"Praise God," somebody says.

"That dog is laying right over there," Granpa T says, and he points.

All the heads turn.

That dog lifts up his head and looks back at the people. I swear he looks like he's about to cry.

Granpa T says the dog's got a broke leg. He says it's in pain. He says it's hungry.

The dog puts his head back down. He closes his eyes. He turns his face toward the wall.

"That dog is one of God's creatures," Granpa T says. "We hurt him, and we don't have the money to help him. So how's this story going to end? How are we going to help that dog—like the good Lord says we ought to?"

"Sweet Jesus," somebody sings out in the back.

The preacher says, "How are we going to help Brother Roberts?"

And Mr. Nelson from the country stands up and he says his daughter works for a veterinarian and he'll help us get the dog there in his truck. And Mrs. Washington with the nephew in Iraq stands up and she says she can give a dollar to help pay. And then other people stand up and say they can, too, and before you know it, somebody's passing a plate and the dollar bills are rolling in and we're all singing again and I'm thinking maybe God does make his own plan, but so far it looks pretty much the same as mine.

3

After church, Mr. Nelson carries the dog off in his truck, but just before he drives away, I get a chance to whisper in that dog's ear not to worry because I got a plan. Of course I don't tell anybody else about my plan. I just lay in bed that night while Tanya's singing herself to sleep and cross my fingers and try to figure out what to do next.

In the morning, I head off to school as usual. I get tired of going to school, especially toward the end of the year. They got the Jazz Fest going on out at the racetrack. They got the flowers blooming all over the yards. They got that breeze coming straight off the river and drifting all over the house when we open up the windows. You can hear the ships blowing their horns and the birds singing in the trees. To tell the truth, that just ain't the time to be sitting in a little bitty desk. That's the time to be outside.

We're all sitting there after lunch trying to pay attention, and it ain't working. That boy Rusty two seats over is falling asleep. His eyes are half shut and his mouth is drooping open. Somebody accidentally-on-purpose drops a book. Everybody jumps and the girls scream. Finally the teacher says, "Okay, enough of that," and starts to hand out paper to draw on.

I feel like making an airplane and flying it straight out the window—with me on it.

But I don't do that. I wait.

Then he says, "This is free drawing time. Draw something you love."

And I think, *If it's free, why do we have to draw something we love? Why can't we draw something we hate?* But I don't say that. I pick up my pencil, and I get ready to draw but I've got some problems.

The first problem is I ain't a good drawer. Jamilla was a good drawer but she's gone. If she were here, she would get me started on whatever it is I'm going to draw—which is the second problem.

What am I going to draw?

J-Boy is sitting next to me like always. He's too old for this class but here he is anyway.

"What are you going to draw?" I whisper.

"I ain't drawing nothing," he says.

"You're a lazy fool," I say.

He shrugs up his shoulders.

"I'm going to draw a dog," I say.

"So you love dogs?"

"I love *my* dog."

"You ain't got a dog."

"I'm going to get one."

"How?"

"I got a plan."

"Who's the fool now?" he says, and puts his head down on his desk.

•◆•

That afternoon, we go visit the dog at the vet's but the vet won't let us see him. He says the dog is pretty bad off. He's getting him ready for surgery. He says that dog's leg is broke so bad he can't save it. He says he's got to cut it off.

Tanya's sitting there with her eyes all big and round, and when he says, "Cut it off," tears swell up like an overflowing gutter and come rolling all down her cheeks.

Mama looks at her and says, "Don't take on, now. It's for the best."

When we get home, Granpa T's sitting in the front room with the baby riding up and down on his knee and the TV going.

Mama says, "I told you he needed a nap."

Granpa T says, "He ain't sleepy."

Mama snatches up the baby and stomps off up the stairs.

Granpa T looks at Daddy and says, "What's wrong with that woman?"

Daddy says, "It's the dog. He's got to have his leg cut off."

Granpa T says, "Whoo-ee," and shakes his head. "How is a dog going to manage with only three legs?"

I sit down and open my book bag. I pull out my picture. I'm looking at it and looking at it. I think I did a pretty good job even if I did do it all by myself. It don't look alive but anybody can see it's a dog. There's only one thing wrong with it. It's got four legs.

•◆•

We go back two days later and that big old dog is laying in a wire cage with a big blue plastic cone around his neck, his half-leg all wrapped up in bandages, and his ribs still looking like a piece of black corduroy cloth laid over a frame.

When we walk in, he lifts up his head and cocks it to one side like he's thinking to himself, *I've seen that boy before*.

"What's that blue thing around his neck?" I say.

"It's a collar," the doctor says, "to keep him from worrying his wound."

"Why would he want to do that?"

"He's a dog. That's what dogs do."

"Why is he all penned up?"

"To keep him resting," the doctor says. "Just for a day or two."

Daddy's standing in the door watching us. "What happens then?" he asks.

"Then he needs a home," the doctor says.

"He ain't a little dog," Daddy says. "He needs a home with a big yard."

"We don't have too many of those in the city," the doctor says. "He'll have to make do with something else."

"We're all making do," Daddy says. He heaves a sigh, and I know he's thinking about the car that's making a funny noise and that stack of letters I saw by the telephone and the lady at school who said I need glasses if I'm going to do my best next year.

I'm standing there beside the cage. That dog pokes his nose at the wires and starts whining. I reach through and rub his head real soft. He quiets right down and closes his eyes.

"Is he ever going to get well?" I say.

The doctor nods. "He's weak because he's old and he hasn't been eating right, but once he stands up and starts getting around, he'll be okay."

"How is he going to manage with only three legs?"

"He'll be fine. He just needs somebody to look after him while he heals and to love him when he's well."

"And to feed him," Daddy says. "And take him on walks and clean up his business."

"That's true," the doctor says.

"That's money," Daddy says. "Come on, son. We've got to go."

When I take my hand off the dog, his eyes pop open and he lifts up his head. He's watching us the whole way down the hall and when I raise my hand to wave good-bye, I swear I see his tail go *thump* again.

•◆•

That night Granpa T's sitting on the porch drinking a beer, and when I finish up my homework, I go out and I sit down beside him.

"That dog's getting better," I say. "The vet says he's going to be able to get around on three legs just fine."

Granpa T don't say nothing. The streetlight flips on and starts buzzing.

"He's going to need a home soon. Somebody's got to look after him while he heals. Somebody's got to help him learn to walk again. Got to take care of him extra good because he's a special dog."

Granpa T takes another sip.

"I want a dog," I say. "A real dog. Not just a picture."

Granpa T sets down the can and looks out at the street. It's pretty dark so there ain't much for him to see.

"I want a dog," I say again, "but Daddy says a dog costs too much to feed."

"What about a chicken?" Granpa T says. "I had a chicken once. When the new ones hatched, my mama pointed and said, 'You want a pet? That one's yours.' I named it Henny Penny and I raised it up from a ball of yellow fluff. I talked to it. It clucked back. It used to scratch around the back steps. It came wobbling out when I called."

Granpa T takes another sip and looks down at me. "So what do you say to a chicken?"

"I don't want a chicken. I want a dog. I want that dog."

Granpa T sets down the can and shakes his head. "That ain't a little dog. He eats a lot."

"I'll sell my Game Boy."

Granpa T picks up the can and takes a long drink.

"I've already talked to J-Boy down the street," I say.

"Is he that big boy who used to come sniffing around when Jamilla was staying here after school?"

"Yeah. I guess so."

"You still play with him sometimes?"

"We don't play," I say. "We just pass the time."

Granpa T looks at me and then he nods. "That's what I meant," he says.

"J-Boy says he'll buy it. He says he's got the money already. He says he'll buy all the games, too."

"You'd really do that?" Granpa T says. He's shaking the beer can. It's empty. "You'd sell that Game Boy?"

I take a deep breath. "I already did it." I reach in my pocket and I pull out money. A lot of money.

"Today," I say, "in school."

We're sitting there looking at my hand all stuffed full of money.

"I want a dog," I say. "I want that dog."

Granpa T stands up. Way up high in the trees, the frogs are screaming. Across the street, the lady's air conditioner comes roaring on.

"I plan on naming him Buddy," I say, "because that's what he'll be, my buddy."

I shove the money back in my pocket. I look up and there's

Granpa T looking down at me in the dark evening. Behind him is the big old sky all full of stars. I cross my fingers.

"I'll go talk to your daddy," Granpa T says, and eases on inside.

4

We bring Buddy home that Saturday morning.

When we pull up in the car, there's Mama, standing on the front porch with her hands on her hips. She says, "Well, I never—" and then she stops. "A three-legged dog," she says, then she turns around and goes inside the house.

Tanya's standing in the door with all her teeth showing in a grin and a ponytail sticking straight up on top of her head.

"What's that he's got around his neck?" she says.

"That keeps him from licking his cut."

"Why would he want to lick his cut?"

"He's a dog, you fool. What do you expect?"

Daddy lifts Buddy out of the car and carries him around the house to the backyard where we have a shed leaning up against the pecan tree. I fluff up the old army blanket Mama gave me and Daddy lays Buddy down right on top.

Buddy gives a little yip when he hits that blanket and pushes around with his front feet like he wants to get away but he can't move.

"Your mama's going to need you in the house after a while," Daddy says.

Buddy's poking his nose around in that blanket smelling everybody who's ever touched it, and that's a lot of people.

I sit myself down right beside him. "It's okay, boy," I tell him. "It's okay now."

"You hear me, son?"

I look up and there's Daddy with his arms crossed over his chest and his eyebrows twisting down toward his nose.

"Yes, sir. I heard you."

Daddy walks out and before he even gets to the house, Buddy's finished smelling the blanket. His ears are standing up tall and he's looking around like he's wondering what might jump out at him from behind all the stuff piled up in that shed.

"Ain't nothing in here," I'm saying. "Just old junk we ain't thrown away yet."

Buddy looks at me like he's not so sure. Then he's checking

out the shed again. His eyes are flicking back and forth from the lawn mower to the rake to the torn-up window screen to the stack of paint cans to the rotten box of floor tiles

"So do you like it here?" I'm saying. "Does it suit you?"

I'm leaning around trying to see his face in that collar when all a sudden he turns around to check me out again. I straighten up and he tilts his head to one side.

"So what do you think?" I say. "Are you wondering what kind of boy it is that would bring you to a place like this?"

His mouth is hanging open and the tip of his tongue is rolling out one side. He's going, "Heh, heh, heh," when he breathes.

He's looking at my face and my feet. He's looking at my hands to see what I might be holding but there ain't nothing there.

"Do you think I look like I can take care of you?"

He don't say nothing.

I reach out and pet his head. He gets still.

"So what are we going to do with a three-legged dog?"

I look up and there's Granpa T standing in the door with Tanya tippy-toeing around the corner right beside him. Buddy snaps his mouth shut and lays his head down. I rub his side and feel those ribs sticking up like the rails on the train track.

"Y'all ain't going to do nothing with him," I say. "He's mine."

All a sudden, Buddy starts whining and turning his neck every which way trying to rub that collar off.

"That ain't good," Granpa T says.

"Stop that, Buddy." I put my hand back on his side. "Stop that, now."

Buddy takes his white paw and pushes at the collar a little, then flops his head back down. He rolls his big old eyes up at me and I think it's just as well he can't talk.

"He don't act like a happy dog right now," Granpa T says.

"He will be," I say. "He's just getting used to being here. He's going to find out I'll take such good care of him he can't help but be happy."

Granpa T's just standing there nodding. He looks at the bowls I found for Buddy. He looks at the great big bag of food stuck in the corner.

"I see you're going to give it your best shot," he says.

"Just give me a little time," I say.

"Can I pet him?" Tanya pipes up.

I look over at Tanya, standing there wearing those plastic, high-heeled shoes with big old pink bows on the toe. "He's mine," I say. "Can't nobody pet him but me."

Tanya's shoulders go all droopy, and her thumb starts heading for her mouth.

So I say, "Oh, all right. You can pet him some."

She comes in and squats down beside him with her knees up to her shoulders and her hands on her knees. She sticks out her hand real easy. Buddy don't move.

"Will he bite me?"

"Are you crazy?"

"He's got big teeth."

"Those are dog teeth."

She touches the top of his head with just her fingertips. He lifts up a little and she snatches back her hand. He sniffs her shoes. Then all a sudden, he sticks out his tongue and licks one of those bows.

Tanya jumps up screaming and hollering. Lucky for her, Granpa T grabs her before she falls over.

"Have you lost your mind?" I say. "Go on now. That's enough. He's tired."

So they leave and I stretch out beside Buddy on the blanket.

"Don't worry about her, Buddy," I say. "You ain't her dog. You're mine. And I ain't going to let her bother you. I promise."

He puts his head on my stomach, collar and all, and it feels warm and heavy.

"It's just you and me now, Buddy," I say.

I'm resting my hand on his side and laying there looking

up at the tin roof. The sun's coming in through that dirty old window on the front of the shed and I think someday I ought to clean it up so Buddy can get better light when the door is shut.

The birds are singing outside, and I can hear Baby Terrell crying in the house.

"I've got to go inside in a while," I say, "but I'll stay as long as I can."

He shifts his head a little but he don't answer.

"If you want me to," I say, "I can tell you a story."

Somebody's driving down the street with his music blasting. When the music's passed, I lift up my head.

Buddy's big old eyes are watching me and waiting.

•◆•

It ain't hard to take care of Buddy. He lays there waiting for me in the morning when I come in to fill his bowl and pour his water. His chin is resting on his paws. His eyes are half-closed and barely moving back and forth while he watches me fluff up his blanket and clean up his business.

"Are you doing okay this morning?" I say. "Do you like that collar any better? Is your leg hurting you? Are you tired of laying there yet?"

I rub him on his head and I lean down and put my nose

between his ears and I smell that old leaf smell and the plastic collar, too. He lifts up his tongue and licks my chin and the spot stays cool for a long time.

On Monday all day long at school the teacher is going on and on about something but I don't know what it is because all I'm thinking about is Buddy. At the end of the day, we have an assembly where girls do flips and cheers, and then we all stand up and say the Pledge of Allegiance, and finally the day's over.

I'm throwing my book bag over my shoulder in the hallway and there's J-Boy watching one of those flip girls walking out the door carrying a gym bag and a sweater.

I pull up beside him, and out the door we go.

"I got the dog," I say. "I named him Buddy."

He don't answer.

"I'm going to paint his name on his bowls. I'm going to use that model paint from those airplanes I made at Christmas. I'm going to—"

J-Boy is still looking at that girl.

"If you keep staring at her you're going to burn a hole in her backside."

J-Boy looks at me like he's about to say something but he don't.

The girl turns the corner so I figure maybe now he can think. "Are you learning those games?" I say.

"What games?"

"Those Game Boy games."

"Some."

We're standing in line to get on the bus. All the kids are pushing and shoving and can't nobody get on. You'd think they don't even want to get home from school. Finally, the driver straightens them out and we start moving.

J-Boy's looking the other way again. "J-Boy," I say, and he turns around. "Why you ain't been by the house in so long?"

He shrugs.

We're finally climbing up the bus steps.

"Come by and see my dog," I say, and take a front seat as usual.

"Maybe," J-Boy says, and passes on down the aisle. He high-fives two brothers from the high school and sits down behind them.

I turn around and look out the window. The stores and churches and houses roll on by. The oak trees are spreading out their shady arms. On the corner, a little kid is sucking a snow ball and holding his mama's hand.

But I ain't thinking about them. I've decided I ain't waiting anymore for Jamilla to write me. I've decided I'm going to write her first. In my mind, I'm already writing that letter. "Dear Jamilla," my letter will say. "Guess what. I have a dog."

•◆•

That very afternoon I write that letter and Mama sticks it in the mail. Then I fix up two bowls with Buddy's name on them. Buddy lays there the whole time watching me paint. Every once in a while his tail flicks and he grunts and moves around like he wants to get up. When the bowls are done, I try to help him. I get my hands up under him. I lift and he flops right back down. I say, "It's okay, Buddy. You just ain't strong enough yet."

Then I lay down beside him and he puts his head on my stomach and I tell him stories. He listens to every word. Mama goes hollering for me and I tell Buddy, "Where does she think I'm at? She knows I'm right here with you."

The next day I feel like I can't hardly sit there in school all day long. After about a thousand years, I finally get home. Mama says I have to bag three dozen pralines and I might as well get it done before I start messing with the dog. When I get out to the shed, Buddy's laying there waiting for me just like I knew he would be. We talk until dark. Then Mama makes me come inside to eat, but that's okay because Buddy's sound asleep.

The next day I try to listen to the teacher, but it's hard. I'm about to fall asleep. Eventually the teacher says tomorrow we're going to start studying New Orleans. He says we're lucky to live here and it's the best city in the world. I'm thinking that's all just fine but when is this day ever going to end. Then all a sudden the bell rings and I want to jump out of my seat singing, "Hallelujah!" but I don't do that. I just hop on the bus and head on home.

Daddy gives me a piece of wood from behind the shed, and Mama says I can use the leftover paint from when we did the kitchen last summer. It's yellow and white, and I think that's just about right. I saw that board off straight on both ends, and I paint the whole thing white. Then I paint BUDDY'S HOUSE with the yellow, real careful, in big square letters. It don't show up as good as I want, so I take the blue from the model paints and I outline the letters. It looks perfect.

Granpa T helps me nail it up over the door to the shed and we stand back and take a look.

"It all worked out," I say.

"What worked out?"

"My plan. I got a dog."

"Yep." Granpa T nods his head. Then he slaps me on the back and starts tee-heeing. "So. I guess you must be about the happiest boy in the world," he says. "Because there's one thing I can tell you for sure. A dog is way better than a chicken."

5

But I ain't happy because Buddy ain't happy, and it don't seem like anything I do makes him happy.

When Daddy gets home from work that night, he comes around back and has a look at the sign nailed up on the shed and at Buddy laying there on the blanket and at me sitting there rubbing Buddy's side.

"Has he moved yet?" he asks, and I shake my head. Then he goes to sit on the front porch with Granpa T and they drink a beer.

Mama comes out and tells me I need to come inside and do my homework. I say I'm busy with Buddy. She says when Jamilla was here she could count on me to get it done before dark. I say she can count on me by myself now, and besides I don't have any. Mama says, "Hmph," and looks down at

Buddy. "That dog's fur looks like a rat's nest," she says, and then goes back inside.

I rub Buddy's head all up under his collar and he don't move. Not even the tip of his tail. I tell him stories until he's asleep. Then I go to sit out front with Granpa T and Daddy.

Everybody's outside taking in the cool of the evening and talking back and forth from their porches. They're talking about work and ball games and how those boys down the street finally crossed the line and got what they deserved and whether Brother James is going to preach one of those "empty your pockets" sermons again for old lady Jenkins who just broke her hip.

And then one of the neighbors sings out, "Hey, Li'l T, where is that ugly, old, three-legged dog?"

And everybody laughs, like it's funny or something.

•◆•

The next day when I get home from school I get an old brush out of the bottom drawer in the bathroom and I go to work on him.

He lays real still and I start at his head. I can't get that fur around his caterpillar scar to lay straight but the fur on his neck lays down softer and softer the more I brush it. I work the brush up under the collar a little and Buddy stretches back his head so I can get way up under his chin.

"You like that," I say, and I swear he smiles.

Up under his stomach, some little wads of fur are still hanging on. I get Mama's sewing scissors and start cutting them out. Buddy half sits up and tries to watch.

"You can't see with that collar," I say. "And anyway, you got to lay down."

He eases back down and I start brushing again. He's watching my face and I'm talking to him.

"You think I'm crazy?" I'm saying. "Giving a dog a haircut? Brushing him with a hairbrush?"

When I run that brush over his sides, I feel the ribs—*bumpity-bump*—and Buddy's eyes start drooping shut.

"You've got to eat up, Buddy," I say. "We've got to make you fat. You've got to get strong."

Then I start to brush near his cut-off leg and he lifts his head up sharp and makes a low sound deep in his throat.

I stop right there. "Did you growl at me?" I just sit there for a minute and look at him.

He looks right back like he knows he's crippled now and it hurts and he feels like a fool with that great big collar going around his head.

Then he lays his head back down and I reach out to rub his nose, but he turns his face away.

I go back to brushing his neck. I don't know what else to do.

"That's all right," I say. "We can just wait on that. There ain't no hurry. You ain't heading for a beauty contest."

"Well, *that's* a good thing!"

I turn around and there's Granpa T, standing in the doorway again.

"He sure ain't winning a beauty contest. He's ugly as sin."

"He's beautiful, Granpa T. You're just blind."

"Maybe," Granpa T says, and eases on in. "But could be you're too crazy in love to see how ugly he is."

"Buddy don't think I'm crazy. He's glad he's living here with somebody'll brush his fur and fill up his bowl."

I don't tell Granpa T, but I ain't sure that's true.

"Granpa T," I say, "why do you think he won't stand up?"

"He's only got three legs, you fool," Granpa T says. "What would you do if you only had one?"

"That vet says he ought to be getting up any day."

Granpa T squats down by Buddy. Buddy moves his head just barely enough to see Granpa T. He don't bother to lift it up. Granpa T lays his hand on the top of Buddy's head and stretches Buddy's eyes way open. That caterpillar eyebrow wiggles up Buddy's forehead and Buddy looks straight up at

Granpa T. His eyes are so dark, so brown, so soft looking. Granpa T lets go and the eyebrow slides back down. Buddy closes his eyes again and I swear he heaves a sigh.

"I think he likes you," I say.

"He likes anybody who'll be nice to him," Granpa T says, and rubs his finger on the caterpillar scar. "He's lucky he ain't blind."

"What do you think he thinks," I say, "waking up and there ain't no leg where there used to be one?"

Granpa T shrugs.

"Do you think he's scared?"

"Are you scared, Buddy?" Granpa T says, almost like he's talking to Baby Terrell.

Buddy opens his eyes.

"What are you scared of?" Granpa T says. "You've got Li'l T now. You've got this fancy shed to live in. You're laying on one of my old blankets."

Buddy lifts up his head.

"You're ugly as sin," Granpa T goes on. "You're ugly as sin and you stink."

Buddy's ears are standing up. His mouth pops open. He starts going, "Heh. Heh. Heh. Heh. Heh."

"Why don't you stand up, dog?" Granpa T says. "Come on, get up."

Buddy's tail is swishing back and forth on the floor. He looks from Granpa T to me and back again.

Granpa T stands up. "Come on. Get up."

Buddy raises himself up on his front feet.

"Ain't it time?" Granpa T says. "Ain't you strong enough?"

Buddy's whining and whimpering. His mouth looks like he's trying to smile but he can't quite do it.

"Come on, dog." Granpa T is moving toward the door. "Don't you want to see what's going on out here?"

Buddy stretches his feet out like he's trying to drag himself to Granpa T.

"Rrrp!" Buddy says. "Rrrp, rrrp!"

"Come on, Buddy. Come on, boy." Granpa T's standing at the door. He's holding one hand out to Buddy and waving the other one out the door.

And then Buddy lets out a little moaning sound and he lays back down and he turns his head toward the wall and he rests his nose on his paws.

•◆•

When we take him to the vet for his checkup, the vet says his cut has pretty much healed, and he takes off that collar. I'm standing there rubbing Buddy's neck, feeling all the way down to the skin where that old collar's been wrapped around him. Buddy is half sitting up with his tongue hanging out of his mouth and looking like he remembers everything about this place, especially that old cage and how he woke up without one of his legs.

Then the vet asks how he's doing about getting around.

I can't even look at the vet. "He ain't stood up yet," I say.

"Not at all?" the vet says.

"Not where I saw him."

The vet gives Buddy a hard look. He feels all around under Buddy's belly. Buddy gives him a look like if he does that too much more, Buddy just might take out a little piece of his hand.

Then the vet gives him a little whomp on the behind and says, "There's nothing wrong with him. It's time for him to get up, even if you have to force him."

When we get home, Daddy says this is the last time he's carrying Buddy. He puts him down on the blanket and leaves out.

Buddy lays there like he ain't never going to move again.

"What's wrong, Buddy?" I say. "Why ain't you happy here?"

Granpa T is standing there in the door and looking in.

"He's old," Granpa T says. "Maybe he's just too tired. Maybe he's been knocked down so many times, he just ain't got the heart to get up anymore."

"So you're saying he wants to die?"

"Aw, no! He's a dog! He don't want to die! I'm just saying maybe he's too tired to live. Look at his eyes. You ever seen any eyes look tireder than that?"

I look at Buddy's eyes. They look big and sad and tired. But they don't look *that* tired.

"Granpa T," I say, "that's the stupidest thing I ever heard. That's the craziest, stupidest, wrongest, dumbest thing I ever heard in my entire life!"

"Probably so," Granpa T says. "Ain't the first time I said something dumb." He gives Buddy a good hard look then looks at me. "Your mama's cooking red beans," he says. "Don't stay out here too long." Then he turns around and heads on inside.

"He's crazy, ain't he, Buddy. He's crazy and stupid and dumb."

I'm rubbing the place that collar used to be. Buddy's laying still as a stone and breathing soft and low.

"Right, Buddy?" I say, but Buddy don't say nothing.

6

Tanya wakes me up that night screaming. Granpa T's banging the door downstairs and cussing, and Mama comes whipping into the room like her hair's on fire, and Baby Terrell starts up in his crib, and Tanya's sitting up in the bed next to mine screaming.

"What is wrong?" Mama yells, and then Tanya stops and I can hear the rain coming down like a waterfall on the porch roof outside the window.

"I had a dream," she says, "and Buddy died."

"That dog," Mama says, and rolls her eyes. She reaches around Tanya and hugs her up, and Tanya's kind of crying a little, and Daddy comes limping into the room carrying Baby Terrell.

"What's wrong?" he says.

"Bad dream," I say, and the thunder rolls.

Daddy sits down on my bed holding Baby Terrell, who's smelling like a wet diaper.

"I think I broke my toe," Daddy says.

And then Granpa T hustles in the door and says, "What the blue blazes is going on?"

"Bad dream," I say again.

Granpa T looks over at Tanya. The way Tanya's hair is standing out all over her head, she sure looks like she had a bad dream. "What were you dreaming about?" he says.

Tanya's digging her fists in her eyes and Mama's rubbing her back and then Tanya hiccups and she says, "Buddy."

"We're all tearing around the house in the dark because you're dreaming about that dog?" Granpa T says.

Tanya nods. "He died," she says, and the lightning flashes all over the room.

"In your dream," I say.

"For true," she says, and looks at me with her great big old, wet eyes. Then they start overflowing again. "He couldn't never stand up and so he died," she says. "And he grew angel wings and flew up, and we were all standing on the ground watching."

"That ain't scary," I say, looking out the window toward where the shed is.

"I ain't finished," she says. "And then a hand came out the sky. A giant hand. And it snatched him up and whisked him off into the clouds."

Mama hugs Tanya up so tight, Tanya says, "Umph."

"That's the hand of God," Mama says. "He took Buddy to dog heaven."

Tanya's tears are starting up again. "But the hand was scary," she says. "And now Buddy's gone."

"It was a dream," Daddy says. "Buddy's sleeping in the shed." Daddy looks out the window. "He's in a dry place for a change. He's a happy dog tonight."

"He's dead," Tanya says. "He's gone, gone, gone." She's looking down at her hands now and the tears are just rolling down her face.

"That's foolishness," Granpa T says. "You need to be quiet now so your daddy can sleep. He's got to work in the morning. T Junior, go change that baby's diaper and put him back in the bed. Everybody, go back to sleep."

Mama kisses up Tanya real good and pulls the covers up to her chin. She walks out the door and flips off the light. Me and Tanya are laying there in the dark listening to the rain and watching the lightning on the wall.

I'm thinking about Buddy laying in the dark outside. That shed's dry, but it's got a tin roof and when it rains, it's so noisy you can't hardly hear the thunder.

"He didn't never stand up?" I say real quiet.

"No," Tanya says. "And then a big hand came."

"Do you think Buddy could die from laying down?"

"He already did. And he grew angel wings."

"He ain't dead."

"I saw it. I didn't tell that part. He laid down on his side and he closed his eyes and he was still all over. And then his whole body started to twinkling like a holy spirit was in it and then, *boom*, he was on his feet and he had angel wings."

"You dreamed it."

"I saw it. He's dead."

I sit up in my bed. "You're just a baby. You can't tell the difference between for true and dreaming. You *dreamed* he's dead!"

"I saw it! With my own eyes!"

Daddy busts open the door. "Y'all be quiet. We're trying to go to sleep now."

"She says—"

"Be quiet. I mean it." Daddy slams the door. The dark fills up the room. I hear Tanya breathing all jaggedy next to me. In my mind I see Buddy laying on that green army blanket. He's got it all pushed into bumps and hills. He's got his nose resting on his front feet. His sides are going in and out with breathing. And then in my mind, his sides stop going. Everything freezes up. There ain't no twinkling. He turns to stone. And then he's gone.

•◆•

In the morning it's still raining so hard Daddy can't go to work. The TV says schools are closed. They've got flooding up on Claiborne Avenue and the street out in front of the house is a river. I dress and find an umbrella while Mama is still looking in the refrigerator for Baby Terrell's bottle. Daddy says to go see if we got a paper, but I ain't listening. I'm out the back door and splashing through the puddle at the foot of the steps. I'm standing at the shed where that sign says BUDDY'S HOUSE like it's so proud or something, and then I'm opening the door.

I'm opening the door and—

And there's Buddy, standing up on three legs. He's standing there all by himself with his white foot in his water bowl and that old blanket all gathered up under his feet and his tail just a-going. That caterpillar eyebrow is cocked to one side, and he's grinning straight at me.

"Rrrruuff!" Buddy says.

I scream and Tanya comes running outside holding her doll by the hair and splashing through the rain.

"He's dead?" she's yelling. "I saw it! He's dead!"

"He ain't dead," I say. "He's alive! And he's standing up!"

Then we're both standing there looking at Buddy.

"Ruff!" Buddy says. "Ruff, ruff!" His ears are standing up on his head and he's grinning like he's prouder of himself than he's ever been in his life.

"But there ain't no wings," Tanya says. "Mama! Mama! Come see."

And here comes Mama, right through the rain with the baby on her hip and a dishrag in her hand, and she says, "Well, I'll be."

And by the time Daddy and Granpa T get outside, Buddy's starting to walk. He hops and steps and hops and steps and then he's standing right in front of me. He reaches up his nose and pokes it in my stomach, and it tickles and I laugh, and I sing out, "Hallelujah!"

And then I get down on my hands and knees. I hug him around the neck. His fur is warm and soft, and he's smelling like those old, wet leaves again. He's shaking all over and his tail is whapping against that torn-up screen propped beside the door.

I lean back and I look in his eyes. "You're my buddy," I

say, and he's licking my nose and my mouth and my eyes and going, "Ruff, ruff!" in my ear, and I'm laughing so hard I fall backwards into the rain and I look up at the sky and I swear I see that old sun just starting to break through.

7

We can't let Buddy out of the shed that first day because everything is too wet, but come Saturday, I open that door in the morning and I say, "Today is your day, Buddy. Today you get to come outside."

He pokes his nose out the door and his ears go *prp!*—standing straight up on the top of his head. He looks around at the tree waving its leaves and at the top of the fence where the cat's claw vine is busting out with yellow flowers, and he starts barking up a storm, standing there with his nose pointing at the tree like he's trying to show me something.

"That's just squirrels," I say. "Ain't nothing new."

He looks at me like he wants to make sure I know what I'm talking about, and then he starts exploring. He's got his own way of walking. His one back foot has to do double time to keep up with his two front feet. He's slow and wobbly, but he gets where he's going.

First, he hobbles over to where the fence meets up with the shed and he starts sniffing at the ground, poking his nose at every stick that fell out of the trees, cruising across that half-dead grass to check out the pecan tree, pushing a rotten old pecan along the ground. Then he snugs up next to the tree, walks in a circle twice, and lays himself down in a spot of dirt between two roots sticking up out of the ground.

"Is that your place, Buddy?" I say, and he looks me in the eye and goes, "Rrruff," and I guess that means, "Yes, it is, and don't bother me when I'm laying here."

About that time Daddy bangs open the back door and leans halfway out. "It's Saturday," he yells.

"I know that."

"You know what it means?"

I can't help it. I roll my eyes.

"Don't you roll your eyes at me."

"I ain't rolling my eyes. And I know I'm supposed to mow the yard. But there ain't hardly any grass."

"There's enough. And the front yard needs it bad."

Ever since we moved into Granpa T's house, cutting the grass has been my job. Granpa T says that's half the reason he asked us to move in. He says after almost forty years going around and around the same yard, he's tired of cutting that grass. He figures he's got a grandson who can do it so it's time to turn over the reins. That first summer he showed me how to gas up the lawn mower and run it back and forth so I don't miss any spots. At first I couldn't pull the cord and Granpa T did it for me, but I finally got the knack and I don't need anybody's help anymore.

I don't get anybody's help either. It's all on me.

So I go over to the shed and roll out the lawn mower. Buddy perks up when he sees me. I'm guessing he probably didn't know that smelly old thing sitting in his house could move. While I'm gassing it up, he limps over and stands right smack up next to me, his mouth hanging open and his eyes watching what I'm doing with the gas can. He jerks his head back when he gets a little whiff of the fumes and then leans down to check out the wheels and sniff the dead grass still stuck on the sides.

"What's so interesting about this old lawn mower, Buddy?" I say, and he looks up at me with his tongue hanging out and his tail wagging.

"When I start this thing up, it's going to blow your ears out and scare you to death."

His tail just keeps on wagging. His mouth looks like he's

grinning and his eyes look like they've got little sparkles dancing around in them.

"Go on back to your place by the tree."

"Rruff!"

"I mean it, Buddy. Go on!" and I fling out my hand and he starts to jump like he thinks I'm throwing something and—*whomp*—he falls over.

"Buddy!" I'm squatting down to help him up, but before I get all the way down, he's standing up again and panting at me like he's waiting for me to do something.

"What do you want, Buddy?" I say.

He takes a step away from me then he takes a step back toward me. He never stops looking at me, his eyes all bright and shiny, his mouth open, and his ears perked up.

"He wants you to throw a ball."

I look up and there's Granpa T in the back door.

"How do you know that?"

"I use my eyes."

"I ain't got a ball."

"Baby Terrell does. Hold on a minute."

Granpa T heads in the house and I look down at Buddy. "What do you know about chasing a ball?"

"Catch!" Granpa T says, and I look up. Before I can figure out what he's doing, Granpa T's already thrown the ball toward the back fence and Buddy's hobbling to it the best he can. Buddy pokes around in the brush against the fence and, sure enough, he finds that ball and brings it straight back to me.

"Well, I'll be," I say, and take it from him.

"Somebody's taught him to play catch," Granpa T says. "He ain't a stray. He used to be somebody's pet."

I look up. The back door slams and Granpa T is gone.

•◆•

It don't take me long to mow the yard. In the front, there are just little squares on either side of the sidewalk because Mama's got bushes and flowers up next to the house and along the fence. And the grass ain't hardly growing yet with the oak tree next door putting so much shade on the yard. In the back, I get it all cut in about two passes while Buddy's standing just inside the shed, barking.

When I get the lawn mower all parked again, I pick up the ball and throw it. Sure enough, Buddy goes after it and brings it back. I throw it again. He brings it back. It's wet with slobber.

His sides are heaving when he tries to draw breath. I lift up my hand to throw the ball again but he heads on over to the pecan tree and sits down.

I sit down beside him and we listen to the sounds all

around us. The squirrels are chucking in the bushes and the birds are chirp, chirping their warnings to each other. There are kids playing in the next block. There are air conditioners running. There are cars and trucks in the streets. The tree frogs are singing in the trees and the people are talking when they walk by. There are sirens and that *beep, beep* sound when working trucks back up.

Buddy lays his head on my leg and I start rubbing him. I touch that old caterpillar scar and he closes his eyes.

"Where did you get that, Buddy?" I say, and his tail goes flip just once.

"Did you run away?" I say. "Were they mean to you?"

The end of his tail flicks a little in the dust.

"Or did they just leave you in the street one day?"

I rub my hand all the way down to Buddy's cut-off leg. He don't even twitch.

"I've heard about people doing that. What kind of people would just leave their dog like that?"

Somebody walking down the street is yelling into his cell phone. Buddy looks up for a second then puts his head back down.

"They didn't love you like I love you, Buddy."

All a sudden a squirrel goes galloping along the top of the fence.

Buddy's up and barking before I can move. He's stepping all over me and his claws are scratching my legs and then—*wham*—down he goes, right in my lap. By the time he gets himself straightened up that squirrel is all the way at the top of the pecan tree.

Buddy's panting in my face and looking up in the tree like he's wondering what I'm planning to do about that squirrel.

And I'm laughing myself silly. "You crazy old dog," I say, and hug him up around the neck. "Can't nobody ever love you like I love you."

"Ruff!" Buddy says. "Ruff, ruff!"

And I swear that dog smiles.

8

Sunday morning when we get back from church, Buddy's barking up a storm again in the backyard.

"What the blue blazes is wrong with that dog?" Granpa T says.

I'm hopping out of the car and running to the back without even unbuttoning my collar, and there's Buddy, standing under the tree and barking at something on the roof of the shed. When he draws a breath, I can hear a squirrel chucking away, telling all his squirrel friends to get out of the way because there's some kind of crazy dog living under the pecan tree now.

"Buddy!" I'm yelling. "Buddy, be quiet. It's just a squirrel!"

But Buddy keeps on barking and that squirrel keeps on chucking.

"Have you lost your mind?" I say. "What's the matter with—?"

And then I see it. Laying on the ground between Buddy's two front feet is a teeny, tiny baby bird. It's so tiny, it don't have any feathers at all. It's just a ball of gray.

"Granpa T! Come see. It's a bird."

And here comes Granpa T, hustling around the corner of the house, cussing Buddy, and complaining about the heat.

All a sudden, Buddy stops barking. There ain't no chucking either.

"Better get it quick before he eats it," Granpa T says.

"Buddy ain't going to—"

"Quick!" Granpa T says, and I look and Buddy's bending down, looking at the bird.

I can't hardly move.

Buddy touches it with his nose and I step forward.

"Don't eat that bird, Buddy," I say.

He looks up, panting and grinning at me.

"What do you want with that baby bird?"

Buddy's ears are all perked up and his tail is wagging.

I hold out my hand and Buddy says, "Rruff!"

Then he backs up in his wobbledy way and stands watching me and Granpa T.

I bend down and pick up the little, bitty bird. He's so

scared he don't move an eye. Buddy's tail is going a mile a minute.

I turn around to Granpa T. "He ain't going to eat no bird," I say. "He's saving it from the squirrels."

"Dogs don't do that," Granpa T says.

"Buddy did," I say.

Granpa T ain't got no answer to that.

•◆•

Tanya says she wants to keep that bird for her pet since I've got Buddy but Granpa T says it's too little to leave its mama and we've got to try to put it back. So we spend the rest of the afternoon trying to get that bird back in his nest. Buddy can't take his eyes off us with the ladder propped up against the trunk and me dangling off a limb halfway up the tree. He's stumbling around under the tree, whining and yipping so much we finally shut him up in the shed. He keeps on whining but at least nobody's going to trip over him.

We look and look and can't find that bird's nest. In the end, we make a new nest with an old basket from out of the shed. Tanya stuffs it full of dry grass and cries when we stick it in some branches where the mama can find it.

"But the squirrels'll come back," she says.

"Can't do nothing about the squirrels," Daddy says. "If

you got a pecan tree in the backyard, you going to have squirrels. Li'l T, let that dog out of the shed before he drives us all crazy."

We're sitting down to eat dinner when Buddy starts up again. We all rush out the back door and there's Buddy, barking at the squirrels. He ain't giving them no polite "ruff, ruff" neither. He sounds like if they get close enough to him he's going to rip their throats out. They're chucking and chucking and he's barking and barking.

We sit back down and Buddy keeps on barking.

"He's keeping those squirrels off that bird," Granpa T says.

"Hmph," Daddy says. "Dogs don't do that."

Granpa T looks over at me, and we smile.

9

Next morning Buddy starts up again. Mama says it's going to drive her up a wall. Daddy says the neighbors are going to start complaining. Granpa T says he's going to have to shoot either the squirrels or the dog if he's ever going to take a nap again. Tanya looks like she's going to start crying and Granpa T says he's just teasing, and can't she tell when he's teasing and when he ain't.

In the end, Mama don't climb the wall, the neighbors don't complain, and Granpa T's gun stays put. By the time school lets out for the summer, Buddy's got all the squirrels scared off and I feel like I'm finally out of prison. No more bus to ride. No more teachers going on and on. No more homework. Mama says for the first week I'm on vacation but after that she's not making any promises.

That first morning I wake up when I please, take care of Buddy, and wander on back into the house where it's cool. After a while I flip on the TV and there's Scooby Doo, driving a car or something, and I think, *I wonder what Buddy would say to that!* Tanya's sitting there with me. When the commercials come on, she says she wants a doll in a wedding dress for Christmas. Mama says don't start talking to her about Christmas and when are we going to get up and make our beds and don't we have anything to do but watch cartoons.

I look outside and there's Buddy, laying in his cool place in the shade keeping an eye on the yard. I go and sit with him.

"You think it's this hot in Chicago?" I ask him. I hold the ball in my hand and toss it up and down but Buddy don't hardly look at it.

"Do you suppose school's out up there, too?" I put the ball down in front of his nose and he pokes it once or twice but he's too lazy to move more than that.

"Do you think they swim in that big old lake in the summertime?"

He swishes his tail around in the dust but he don't move anything else.

"Why do you think Jamilla ain't never answered my letter?"

Buddy looks at me with his caterpillar eyebrow raised up like he wishes he knew.

"I'm going to write her again," I say.

Buddy flips his tail to say he thinks that's a good idea.

"I'm going to tell her how good you're doing."

Buddy lays his head down and closes his eyes. I guess he's had enough of talking.

I just sit there watching him and letting my hand smooth the top of his head over and over. I'm thinking it will be an easy letter to write because there ain't no doubt about it. Buddy's doing better. He's getting around good when he stays inside the yard. His ribs ain't showing near as bad. His bandage is off, and if you look at him right, you forget there are only three legs.

But all that getting well is hungry work. Buddy's eating more and more, and my Game Boy money is almost gone. Something's got to happen, but I don't know what. I don't have anything else to sell and I ain't old enough to get a job. I need another plan.

"What am I going to do, Buddy?" I say, but he don't say nothing. He's so asleep his tail don't even twitch. I lean back against the bark of the tree. I look up. Somewhere behind the leaves is the big old sky.

"You got any ideas?" I say, but the sky don't answer.

•◆•

I ask Granpa T if he'll pay me to mow the lawn and he looks at me and says, "That ain't even funny. Go on, boy, and find yourself something to do."

I ask Mama if she'll pay me to bag up pralines. She says I've lost my mind and leave her alone while she's cooking.

I know better than to say anything to Daddy. That's just asking for trouble.

I sit down by Baby Terrell. I lean up close and say, "Gootchie, gootchie, goo," and he whops me with his toy truck. Tanya yells out to Mama that I'm bothering the baby and then says don't step on her shoes.

Mama leans in the door and says go throw the ball with that dog and I say it's too hot. Mama says well do something and I ask what. She says you better think of something before I think of something for you.

And then Tanya pipes up and says she wants a snowball.

Before you know it, Mama reaches in her purse and pulls out some money and tells me to take Tanya down the street and get her a snowball. "Get one for yourself, too," she says.

So out the door we go.

That sun's beating down on us all the way down the street. Tanya's about to step in an anthill so I push her to one side and she knocks up against somebody's fence and turns around and says, "I'm telling," and I say, "You want fire ants crawling all over your feet?" And she sticks out her tongue at me!

"I ain't never taking you for a snowball again," I say.

"Meanie," she says, and sashays on down the sidewalk like she thinks she's grown.

The lady at the snowball stand has sweat running down her face. Tanya's standing there with her finger in her mouth trying to decide what flavor she wants. I can't hardly stand up, it's so hot.

"Just say bubblegum," I say. "You always want bubblegum."

"Now I want something different," she says, and keeps on standing there.

"Maybe green," she says.

"Mint?" the lady says, and mops the counter.

Tanya makes a face. "Pink," she says.

"Strawberry or cherry?" the lady says.

Tanya's finger goes back in her mouth and I roll my eyes.

"You're holding up the line," I say to Tanya.

Tanya looks around. "There ain't no line."

"I'm the line," I say. "And I'm waiting."

Tanya heaves a sigh. "Bubblegum," she says. "I'll have bubblegum."

"What about you, son?" the lady says.

I've got my mind all made up. I open my mouth to say

strawberry, and then—I shut it. All a sudden, I'm thinking I don't have to buy a snowball. I can save that money. Mama won't ever know.

"Nothing for me," I say.

Tanya spins around. "Well, why are you fussing about me if you ain't getting nothing yourself?"

"That lady's waiting," I say. "You're taking up her time."

I pay for Tanya and put the same amount in my pocket.

All the way home, I'm trying to make a plan. How many times do we have to get snowballs before I can buy another bag of food? What if Tanya tells Mama I didn't get one? Wonder if anybody else wants somebody to take their little kid to get a snowball? I'm trying to do all the numbers in my head. They ain't working out like I want. I'm thinking I need a piece a paper if I'm going to figure all this out.

When we get home, I forget all about the paper. Buddy takes a good, long look at Tanya and decides he better clean her up. He starts licking her face. He's licking her hands. He's licking her legs. He's sniffing her sandal shoes and poking his nose at the leftover paper from the snowball. Tanya's laughing like she's having the time of her life and Buddy starts up barking.

"You crazy dog," Tanya says, laughing so hard she's about to fall over. "I ain't a squirrel!"

Finally I tell Tanya to get inside and clean herself up because she's the worst mess I've ever seen in my life.

I throw the ball for Buddy and he goes to find it. Four times in a row. It's a record. Then he goes over to his bowl and slurps out some water. He looks up at me with his face all wet and drippy.

"You're bad as Tanya," I say, and he wags his tail.

"You ain't got a lick of sense," I say, and he wags his tail harder.

"You ain't even worried about how I'm going to feed you, are you?"

Buddy says, "Rruff!" and I know that means "You'll figure it out Li'l T. I know I can count on you."

10

Saturday morning Daddy shakes me awake bright and early. "You forgot to do your job."

"What job?"

"You're supposed to cut the grass. You ain't run the lawn mower in over a week."

I can't help it. I make a face.

"Just for that," Daddy says, "you can cut Mrs. Washington's grass, too. With her nephew gone she ain't got nobody to do it—and you ain't got nothing else to do."

I look up at Daddy and he's standing there with his arms crossed over his chest. I pull the pillow over my face. "Why do I have to do Mrs. Washington's, too? Why can't somebody else—"

"Just for that you can do it this week *and* next," Daddy

says. "You better quit while you ahead, boy, and get out of that bed."

There ain't nothing for it. I have to do it.

When the grass starts growing in the spring, it ain't so bad. Everything's all fresh and green, the air's even a little cool, and you don't have to mow but maybe once every two weeks. But by the time summer comes, the air feels like a wet rag laying across your face and the mosquitoes are biting all day. You have to do it at least once a week and even then there's so much cut-off grass laying there you have to rake it up and spread it under the bushes. Granpa T keeps saying he's going to get one of those mowers with a bag on the back but there ain't never enough money for that, so I just keep on raking.

When I make it out to the shed, Buddy's standing there waiting for me like he knew I was coming.

"What do you want, Buddy?" I say, and he says, "Rruff!"

I drag the mower out of the shed and gas it up. I yank on the cord and when it starts up, Buddy yelps and hops back into the shed.

"You stay right there," I yell. "I ain't going to be long."

I whip that mower around the yard so fast Baby Terrell ain't even finished with his bottle by the time I'm done.

Buddy comes creeping out of the shed when I start raking up the grass.

"This is a fool thing to do, ain't it, Buddy?"

He's poking his nose in my pile of grass.

"Why people can't let their grass just grow, I don't know."

I rake that grass up under the bushes, sling the rake over my shoulder, and shove the lawn mower through the gate.

Buddy's standing there on his three legs, panting in the heat and wondering what he's supposed to do.

"You stay here, Buddy," I say. "I'll be back."

He sits right down and he waits.

•◆•

Mrs. Washington lives two streets up and around the corner. It ain't that far to walk but it's far to push the mower. I'm already hot by the time I get there and I just get hotter walking around and around in the sun. She ain't got a single tree in her yard. Mama says she won't let any grow there because she's afraid they'll fall over in a storm and crush her house.

I think old people get crazier every year.

When I'm done, I'm about to push through the gate when she opens the door and walks out on the porch.

"I've got a cold drink inside," she says. "You want one?"

I know Buddy's waiting, but I don't ever turn down a cold drink. I roll the lawn mower around to the backyard so nobody will steal it and she opens the kitchen door and lets me into the cool.

Her house is tiny. Her kitchen is just about big enough for two people to stand in. She opens her refrigerator and I step into the hallway.

"What kind do you want?" she says behind the door.

"Have you got a Coke?"

"I do," she says. "Here it is." The door shuts and she stands up and hands me a cold drink. It ain't a Coke. "That's the last one," she says.

I don't know what to do. I pop open the top and take a sip. It's good, but it ain't a Coke.

"Sit down," she says, and points to the front room sofa.

I sit down.

"I've got a letter," she says, and pulls a letter out from under the lamp sitting on the table by the sofa. "From Iraq," she says. "You want to read it?"

What am I supposed to say?

She hands it to me. "Open it," she says. "Read it. Out loud."

"Dear Aunt Mary," it starts out. I look up at her. She's looking at me through her big, thick glasses. All a sudden it dawns on me. She can't hardly see.

She can't see it ain't a Coke. She can't see to read her letter.

I put down the cold drink and start to read all the things her nephew has to say. How he misses this and how he misses that. How the other brothers are good and they're a team. How he's worried about her all alone. How he can't wait to get home. How he's got plans to fix up the kitchen. How he's got to go now but he'll write again soon.

I finish it up and look over at her and she's smiling. "He's a good boy," she says, and stands up. She reaches in her purse and hands me a five-dollar bill. "You didn't think you were mowing for free, did you?" She laughs. "You come back next week. You can read his next letter."

When I get home, Buddy's waiting for me at the gate. I push the lawn mower toward the shed and he's sniffing at the wheels. I roll the lawn mower into its spot and I sit down by Buddy's blanket. He limps over and lays down with his head in my lap. I run my hand across his head. I brush the bristly ends of his caterpillar eyebrow. I pull on his ears and I scratch up under his neck. He turns his head and looks up at me.

"Mrs. Washington's nephew is doing all right," I say. "He sounds happy enough."

Buddy shifts his head a little.

"Maybe I'll join the army," I say. "But I don't want to go to Iraq."

I rub behind Buddy's ears.

"Mrs. Washington's a nice lady," I say. "She gave me five dollars."

I look over at Buddy's food bag. All a sudden, I have an idea, and one more time, I'm making a plan.

11

Granpa T says I can use the mower. Mama says it's all right with her so long as I don't go too far. Daddy says it's fine but I have to pay him some for the gas. Tanya says I can use her markers to make my signs.

The next day I sit down at the table and start making signs. Tanya wants to help, but she still makes some of her letters backwards so nobody can read anything she writes. Jamilla would have been a big help but there ain't nothing I can do about that. So all by myself I make up a whole pile of signs that say I'll mow a lawn for five dollars. I put our phone number on them. Then I start walking the streets looking for houses to leave them at.

Most of the people, I know. I always knock on the door and if nobody answers, I just leave it in the mailbox.

Sometimes somebody comes to the door. At J-Boy's house, his mama comes to the door in her nightgown. I give her the note and she looks at it and says, "Ain't you J-Boy's friend?" and I say, "Yes," and she says do I know where he is and I say no. Then she shuts the door.

By the time I get home, two people have already called and all a sudden, I'm in business.

"What are you going to call your company?" Granpa T says.

"Li'l T's Lawn Mowing Service," I say.

Granpa T nods. "Got a ring to it," he says.

•◆•

The very next day I take the lawn mower out and tell Buddy good-bye and head off down the street. I mow three different lawns. I've got three five-dollar bills sitting in my pocket and every single one of those people said for me to come back next week. I'm rolling my lawn mower back to the house and I'm thinking maybe somebody else has called while I was gone when I look up and I see J-Boy walking up the sidewalk. We ain't talked since school let out.

"S'up?" he says. He don't smile or nothing.

"Not much," I say.

"So are you mowing those lawns?" he says.

I nod. The sweat's rolling into my eyes and I wipe it out.

"That's hard work for slow money," he says.

"Money's money," I say, and look down at the lawn mower. It's got new grass all stuck on the sides. The rubber gripping part under my hands is starting to work loose.

J-Boy takes one finger and rubs it across under his nose. I can't help it. I see he's starting a mustache.

"So where is that dog?" he says.

"He's in the back. Do you want to see him?"

We stand there another second. J-Boy's looking off down the street. He hikes up his pants a little.

"You don't have to if you don't want to," I say.

"I'll come." He follows me through the gate while I'm pushing the lawn mower to the back.

We turn the corner around the house and there's Buddy, standing in the door of the shed, his tail whacking back and forth.

"Hey, Buddy," I say, and drop on my knees in front of him. "You miss me? You miss me, boy?" I'm rubbing his head. He's licking my face. His whole body's shaking, he's so glad to see me. "This is J-Boy," I say to Buddy. "From down the street."

J-Boy's hanging back. His hands are shoved into his pockets.

Buddy's looking up at him and grinning.

"He likes you," I tell J-Boy. "You can pet him if you want to."

J-Boy don't move. He's just looking at Buddy with his eyes squinched up.

"It's okay," I say. "He don't bite."

"Did he get in a fight?" J-Boy says.

I rub my finger across Buddy's scar. "I guess," I say. "That was there when we found him."

Buddy takes one limping step toward J-Boy and J-Boy steps back.

"What happened to his leg?"

"When we hit him with the car, it broke so bad, they had to cut it off."

Buddy's tail is whacking against the door frame so I move over a little bit. Buddy limps along with me and now his tail's free to swing wide.

"He can't hardly walk," J-Boy says.

"He's walking fine," I say. "He just don't go far."

"You sold your Game Boy so you could get that *piece* of a dog?"

I turn around and there's J-Boy with his lip all curled up.

"If I get me a dog," he says, "I'll get me a *whole* dog."

I'm just staring at J-Boy.

"I always knew you were a fool," he says. "Now everybody else knows it, too." He turns around and walks back around the house to the front yard.

I hear the gate squeal and bang when he slams it open. I sit down. I'm smelling the cut-up grass stuck on the lawn mower and the gas fumes leaking out. I'm feeling the little rocks under my butt and the wood behind my back where I'm leaning against the shed.

Then Buddy sticks his cold nose in my ear. He licks my face. He's whining just a little bit. He limps one step closer and lays down with his head in my lap.

My hand goes to his head. I smooth back his fur and he looks up at me with his caterpillar eyebrow cocked to one side. He's waiting for me to talk but I can't think of nothing to say.

12

J-Boy's the fool, of course. Mama and Daddy have been saying it all along and it's for true. As it turns out, I've got one call waiting when I get inside and the very next day when I roll out the lawn mower, Buddy comes limping along with me. He's doing his three-legged walk down the sidewalk and some little kid snickers and I say, "You laugh at my dog and I'll bust your head." That little kid's eyes get all big and he runs inside. Buddy lifts up his tail and watches him run, and I think, *There goes that mowing job.*

While I mow the lawn, Buddy lays down on the sidewalk. He puts his nose on his front feet and he watches me going back and forth, back and forth. When people walk down the street they're cussing at him for laying in the sidewalk. I say, "What do you expect? He's only got three legs." Buddy lifts up his head and watches them walk on and I tell him, "Just you lay back down, Buddy. It's okay to stay right where you are."

When we get home I fill up his water bowl and I rub his ears and we sit in the shed by the lawn mower and we talk.

"If you had four legs," I say to Buddy, "we might walk down to the river. Mama says I can't go that far but if you went with me, she'd have to let me go."

Buddy's tail goes *thump, thump* like he's saying he wishes he could help me.

"We could really throw the ball there. And we'd watch those barges make the turn. Jamilla and me saw that once when we were at the aquarium. Those barges coming down the river go under the bridge so fast you think they're going to whack right into it but they don't. After they pass under the bridge, they've got to swing way wide to one side to get around the bend in the river, and you're just hoping they don't smash into the bank, and they don't. And then you look and you see the other barges coming *up* the river, and you think now, for sure, they're going crash into each other. And you cross your fingers and close your eyes, and when you open them up again, there go the barges, sailing past each other like nothing ever happened. And after that, you look up and down the river, and you can't hardly believe it because here comes a whole bunch more barges, doing it over and over again."

When I stop talking, Buddy thumps his tail like he wants me to go on.

"Where do you think those barges are coming from, Buddy? What do you think they've got in them? What do you think it would be like to ride on one of them? Jamilla said she's going to do that one day. Start maybe all the way at the top of the river and ride all the way down. All the way out to the ocean.

"Where do you think that river starts, Buddy? I know it ain't Chicago. But it can't be too far from there.

"And what do you think the ocean looks like, Buddy? I've seen pictures and I've seen movies, but I ain't never seen the real thing. Do you think it's scary, Buddy? All that water moving all the time? And what about mountains? What about hills? We ain't even got hills in New Orleans. We've got swamps and we've got alligators and we've got roaches, but we ain't got hills."

Buddy ain't moving. He's asleep.

"Do you think I ought to stay in New Orleans when I get grown? Do you think Mama would let me go off? What if I go where it gets cold sometimes and—"

Buddy jumps and wakes himself up.

"It's okay," I say. "You're coming with me."

He settles his head back on my lap.

"But we can't go now, Buddy. I've got all those lawns to mow and at the end of the summer, there's school all over again."

I heave a sigh and Buddy does, too.

"But guess what Daddy says," I go on. "He says, if I've got enough money come August, he'll take me to the store and we'll get a bicycle."

Buddy looks up at me, and I say, "You think I ought to get a red one?"

His tail goes *thump, thump*, and I say, "Okay. Red it is."

•◆•

One day Mama sends me down the street for a gallon of milk. She gives me a five-dollar bill and says hurry, so I don't take Buddy. I hear Baby Terrell squalling in the kitchen and I figure Mama's about to lose her mind, so I run all the way to the store. I grab the milk out of the cooler and slap that five-dollar bill on the counter and then I hear Brother James's voice behind me.

"Is that Li'l T?" he says.

I turn around real polite. "Yes, sir."

"You still got that three-legged dog?"

"He's named Buddy."

Brother James nods and smiles. "That's a good name for a dog."

"You want this money or not?" says the lady behind the counter.

"Better take that change," Brother James says. "Can't go wasting money."

I stuff the change in my pocket and Brother James says, "Is it true what I hear about you mowing lawns?"

I nod.

"You think you can mow the church lawn? We got some high grass right about now."

I'm thinking fast. "The church is a long way to push my lawn mower," I say.

Brother James falls out laughing. "We got a lawn mower," he says. "We just don't have anybody to push it. Come over Saturday evening. That way it'll look nice for Sunday."

I pick up the milk but I don't go. "How much I get paid?" I ask.

"Paid!" Brother James says.

I nod.

"This is the church, boy."

"I'm feeding Buddy now," I say, "and I'm saving for a bicycle."

"Five dollars," Brother James says. "And that better be one fine bicycle."

13

Mama and Daddy have a fight about it but Granpa T finally speaks up and says I'm old enough to walk all the way to church by myself. Mama's muttering about maybe Buddy can walk with me, and I say no it's too far for him, and she wraps her hands up in her apron and hollers at Granpa T to turn down the TV before he wakes up the baby, and then she says *somebody's* got to cook some supper and stomps off to the kitchen, and Daddy and Granpa T look at me and say, "What are you waiting for?" and out the door I go.

I'm halfway out the gate before I realize I ain't explained to Buddy. I find him laying in the shade of the pecan tree.

I start rubbing his head. "I can't take you with me to the church, Buddy," I say to him. "You'd be worn out if you walked that far. I'd be carrying you home and I ain't strong enough to do that."

He looks up at me and I'm thinking maybe I can make him a leg. Like those pirates on TV. Maybe I can fix up a stick or something and hook it on the piece of leg still hanging in the back.

But now I got to go mow. Buddy's laying there thumping his tail at me and Tanya walks out the back door.

She comes creeping over and squats down by Buddy. "I'll look after him while you're gone," she says.

"He'll be fine," I say. "He don't need you."

She twists up her mouth and cocks her head to one side. "Meanie," she says.

I ball up my fist and shake it at her. "Meanie yourself," I say. "You leave my dog alone."

She stands up and goes prancing back to the house.

"You watch out for her," I say to Buddy. "She's a girl."

•◆•

Brother James is waiting at the church when I get there. He gives me the key to the shed in back and sure enough there's a lawn mower in there. I get it going and I start mowing. That grass is as high as my knees in places. It chokes up the mower over and over. I'm thanking the Lord it's a tiny little lawn when Brother James comes out and says next I've got to rake up all the grass and stick it in trash bags and then pile them behind the church.

I'm thinking this is a twenty-dollar job, not no five-dollar mow-and-go.

When I'm done, Brother James comes out and looks it over. He says I did a good job. He says I can come back next Saturday—like that's something I might want to do! Then he hands me a five-dollar bill and says, "See you in the morning, son."

I stuff that five-dollar bill in my pocket and I walk home thinking the last thing I'm going to do next Saturday evening is mow that church lawn. I'm thinking about how hot I am and how thirsty I am and how I wish I had a cold drink. I'm thinking about when I grow up I'm going to live where there's snow in the wintertime and frozen-up lakes where you go skating. I'm going to live where the leaves get red and orange in the fall and they got apples on the trees.

I'm thinking I'll be taking Buddy with me on that trip. I'm thinking with all that hot fur he'll be glad to go where it's cold.

I head straight for the back to ask Buddy what he thinks and when I round the corner of the house, I stop in my tracks. I can't believe my eyes.

Tanya's sitting there with Buddy. She's got a great big ribbon tied around his neck in a big old bow. She's got one of those ballerina skirts going around his stomach. She's holding onto one of his front feet and singing how they going to dance the night away.

I start yelling.

Tanya jumps up and starts screaming.

Buddy stands up on his three legs and starts barking.

Mama comes running out the back door and starts hollering.

Granpa T comes right behind her saying, "What the blue blazes—"

"Get away!" I'm yelling. "He's my dog! Get away!"

I'm pulling at Tanya and she's beating on my hands to make me turn her loose. I'm dragging her away and Mama comes running up and she says, "Have you lost your mind?"

And I yell, "Look what she's done!"

"Turn her loose!" Mama hollers.

I drop Tanya's arm and she goes running into the house. I hear her crying inside like somebody's hurt her or something.

Then Daddy comes busting out of the house carrying the baby. He don't say nothing. He hands the baby to Mama. "Go on back to the house," he says to her. "See about Tanya."

Mama's talking to herself all the way back to the door. She lets it bang shut behind her.

Granpa T's standing there looking at Buddy. Buddy's mouth is hanging open and his tongue is hanging out and he's panting in the heat and his caterpillar eyebrow is all cocked up to one side and some people might say he's laughing but I know it ain't so.

"That dog's got the patience of Job," Granpa T says.

"Tanya did it," I say. "She made him look like a fool. Did you hear him barking like that? He can't stand it."

Granpa T squats down and unties the bow. He rubs Buddy around the ears. "You're the ugliest, stupidest-looking dog I've ever seen," he says, and Buddy's tail goes *thump, thump*.

"If J-Boy had seen that," I say, "he'd fall out laughing. He'd say—"

Then I realize Daddy's holding me by the arm. He ain't talking. I look up at him. His face is hard.

Granpa T slides that skirt off Buddy and laughs. "That's a good costume for Mardi Gras, Buddy," he says. "We've got to remember it. Li'l T, did I ever tell you the story about—" Then he looks at Daddy standing there holding me by the arm. "I'll go on back inside now," Granpa T says, and leaves out carrying the clothes.

Then it's just me and Buddy and Daddy standing by the shed. Buddy lays down and it gets awful quiet.

"Did you see your sister's arm?" Daddy says. "She's going to get a bruise."

I don't say anything.

"What do you think I ought to do, son?"

I shrug.

He shakes my arm. "You ain't listening."

"Yes, I am."

"You hurt your sister. What do you think I ought to do?"

"Don't know."

Daddy's real quiet for a minute.

"You want to keep that dog, son?" Daddy says, and all a sudden, I feel something cold running in my stomach.

"Yes, sir," I say real quiet.

"In this family," he says, "we share."

I nod.

"We ain't got much," he says, "but what we got, we share."

"Yes, sir."

"Are you going to share from now on?"

"Yes, sir."

"Go get the stick."

I know where the stick is. It's leaning up behind the shed. I go and get it.

Daddy holds it a minute. "You about to be too big for this," he says. "But I expect I won't be needing it much longer."

"No, sir," I say.

He walks in the shed and I follow him. I lean over. He whaps me. Three times. Then he leaves out.

Buddy comes nosing in. While I'm rubbing my behind, he's whining and poking at my hand. Finally, he lays down on his blanket and I lay down beside him.

"You're my dog," I say.

He lifts up his head and licks my face clean.

14

I mow the church lawn again the next Saturday evening. Daddy says I have to, so I do. Brother James gives me another five dollars even though it don't take even half as long. I stop by the store on my way back. When I get home, Tanya's sitting there singing to Buddy. She's promised she won't dress him up anymore and I've said she can sit and sing to him when I leave out.

"I'm back now," I say.

"I ain't finished my song."

I sit down to wait.

Tanya's got a pretty voice. I ain't going to say it out loud, but it's for true. Except she don't know any songs. She just makes it up as she goes along.

"You're a beautiful dog," she's singing to Buddy.

"You've got great big eyes.
You've got pretty, black fur.
Your tongue hangs out between your teeth when you're hot.
You go 'Ruff, ruff!' when Li'l T comes back.
You look at me when I sing.
You put your head down on your feet.
Your ears go—"

She stops.

She tilts her head to one side and looks at Buddy. Then she starts up again.

"I don't know any words for what your ears do.
They can stand up on their own.
They're pink inside."

"That's enough," I say. "This song ain't never going to end."

She hunches up like she's afraid I'm going to hit her.

"Can't you sing something else? Something that's got an end?"

"'The Eensy, Weensy Spider'?" she says.

"Okay. That's short." I wait all the way through. I see her drawing a breath to start over. "You're finished. Now go."

She hops up and runs inside, and Buddy turns his eyes to me.

I reach in the bag I brought from the store.

"It's a present," I say to Buddy.

He lifts up his head and looks.

"Dog biscuits," I say. I open the box and take one out. I hand it to him. He crunches it between his teeth. He drops it. He picks it up. He's slobbering all over that biscuit until it's completely gone.

I laugh. "Was that good?"

He looks up at me. He's staring at me and panting. I know he wants another one so I throw him another one. He loves those biscuits.

I'm thinking, *What do I want with a bicycle? I'm getting more biscuits next week*. And I throw him another one.

•◆•

I start getting biscuits for Buddy every week on my way home from mowing the churchyard. I go with Mama when she's making groceries and I get him his regular food plus a rubber bone that squeaks when he bites it. First time he bites it, he jumps. Then he bites it again and shakes it. Me and Tanya are laughing at him. He thinks he's putting on a show.

One day I walk all the way to the pet store on St. Claude and Frenchmen Street. They've got birds in cages and rats and kittens and mice and everything. They've got a whole wall of fish swimming around plastic plants. They've got shelves stacked all the way to the ceiling with toys and food.

"What are you looking for, son?" the man says.

"I've got a dog," I say.

"What's he need?"

"Almost everything."

"He got a collar?"

I shake my head.

"He needs a collar."

The man walks to a whole rack of collars. "Is he a big dog or a little dog?"

"Medium."

He lifts up a red leather collar. "Is this one long enough?" He wraps it around in a circle and I think about Buddy and whether it would fit around his neck.

"Yes, sir," I say.

"You got a tag?"

"A tag?"

"You need a tag. You need to put his name on it and your phone number so if he runs off, they can find you."

"Buddy can't run. He's only got three legs."

"He's named Buddy? I've got a tag with that name already on it." He shows me a whole display of name tags.

Sure enough, there's one that says Buddy. It's silver, with the letters already scratched into it.

"I'll take it," I say, and I hand him the money.

When I put it on Buddy, he stands up straight like he thinks he's really somebody's dog now.

"You the man," I say to Buddy.

"Rruff!" Buddy says.

And I think that means, "You, too, Li'l T."

15

By the end of July, I'm about worn out with mowing yards. Some people don't call me anymore. Some people call me twice a week. J-Boy's mama calls me once and I mow the yard, but then she says she don't have the five dollars and she'll send J-Boy with it tomorrow. He don't never come. Daddy says I got to just write that one off and I don't have to go back if she calls again, which she don't.

Mrs. Washington wants me to come inside every time I go. She gives me a cold drink and we read a letter—might be a new one, might be an old one. She don't care. She just picks up one laying in the pile and hands it to me. She's starting to feel happy because her nephew says he's coming home soon.

I'm getting tired of pushing the lawn mower around and

around the yards. I'm getting tired of watching cartoons on the TV. I'm getting tired of hearing Tanya singing.

Mama's always telling me to sit up straight at the table. Daddy's always telling me to chew with my mouth closed. Granpa T's saying how did I get such big feet. Tanya's saying why do I take up the whole sofa when we're trying to watch TV.

Buddy don't say anything. Buddy lays beside me under the tree. I scratch behind his ears. I throw him the ball a time or two. He listens to my stories. When I go inside, I smell him on my hands and I don't want to wash it off.

The days are slipping by and I feel like I'm half asleep most of the time.

Then the next time I go to mow at the church, I can't hardly believe my eyes. Brother James rolls out a brand-new lawn mower with a bag on the back. He shows me how to unhook the bag and dump the cut-off grass in these special new trash bags he bought. That mower whips around that churchyard so fast I feel like it's pulling me instead of me pushing it. I fill up those trash bags before you know it, set them behind the church for trash day, and get home with a box of Buddy treats before I feel like I'm hardly gone.

"Granpa T," I say at dinner that night. "You got to get one of those new lawn mowers. Ask Brother James how much it costs."

"Don't matter how much it costs," Granpa T says. "I ain't spending money on a lawn mower when I got you to do the job."

"Maybe I'll buy it," I say. "Maybe I'll save up my money next summer and get a fancy lawn mower and can't nobody use it but me."

"You have to share," Tanya says. "Daddy said so."

"You want to mow the lawn?" I say.

She gets all quiet.

"You can mow the lawn if you want to," I say.

"Stop it," Mama says. "Now you're teasing her."

I swear the tip of Tanya's tongue is sticking out at me. "Mama," I say, and start to point.

"Your feet are in my way again," Granpa T says.

I put down my hand. I move my feet. We all just keep on eating.

•◆•

Next Saturday I decide to try an experiment. I decide to let Buddy come with me, all the way to the church.

We go slow. He takes a long time, sniffing at the tree trunks and barking at the squirrels. Once, he starts to take off after one but I holler, "Stay!" and he stops just like that and comes limping back and plops himself right down beside me!

"Good dog," I say, and rub up around his ears. "Who taught you that, Buddy? Where are you from?"

Buddy don't say nothing. He just sits there panting in my face and then he takes a little lick and I laugh and off we go again.

It takes us about three times as long to get to the church but I figure it's worth it. I've got somebody to talk to while I do my work. I drag open the shed door and show off that brand-new lawn mower to Buddy. He sniffs its wheels and checks out the bag on the back. While I gas it up, he's poking it with his nose and almost tripping me when I go to put the can away. Then I lay my hand on the cord and he hops to the back of the shed and sits down and waits, his tongue hanging out of his mouth and his ears stretching up to listen.

"Rruff!" he goes when the motor starts. "Rruff, rruff! Rrruff!" But he don't move. He just sits there and barks and waits.

I roll that lawn mower out and I start my circles. After a minute, Buddy peeps out of the shed to watch. When I head to the front, Buddy edges around the corner and sits himself down on the church steps just like he does when we're going house to house. Every time I come close, he lifts up his head and looks at the mower and gives a little "Rruff!" like he's saying, "Good job, Li'l T. Thank you for my food!"

When I'm all done, I go in the back to get those special bags. Brother James bought a wire rack you hook the bag on to hold it open. I'm searching all through that shed and can't find it. I'm saying, "Where did I put that rack last Saturday?" and then I see it, stuck up in the corner and almost invisible in the dark. I grab the rack and the bags, and then I hear Buddy start barking.

Buddy's barking up a storm. He's barking like that churchyard is full of squirrels. He's barking like he's going to tear out every one of their throats twice over. He ain't drawing breath. He's just barking and barking.

I throw down the stuff and I tear around the church to the front, and I see why.

Buddy's standing up on his three legs on the church porch tied to the post with an old piece of rope and two boys are pushing that lawn mower down the street.

"Hey, you!" I yell. "Hey, you!"

They turn around, and I see one of them is J-Boy.

"What're you doing with that lawn mower?" I yell.

They turn back around and keep on pushing.

I start running after them.

"J-Boy," I'm yelling. "J-Boy, what are you doing with that lawn mower?"

Buddy's barking and barking and pulling at that rope.

I'm about to catch up to them.

"Leave that lawn mower alone," I'm yelling. "That's the church's lawn mower!"

Buddy's voice is practically going hoarse with barking.

And then I'm there, and I shove J-Boy off to one side, and he falls down, and that other boy takes off down the street, and J-Boy is laying there on the sidewalk with his forehead bleeding. Then he looks up at me and says things I can't write down.

"Go home," I say, and I watch him get up.

Buddy's still barking on the church porch.

"Be quiet, Buddy," I say.

Buddy stops barking and stands there looking at us like we're just a little bit too far away to suit him.

"I should have shot that dog," J-Boy says. He grabs hold of something under his shirt. "I've got a gun," he says. Then he turns around and walks off down the street. He holds up his hand just before he turns the corner, and I know he ain't giving me no good-bye wave.

•◆•

Daddy shakes his head when I tell him about J-Boy.

Mama says she doesn't care if he's last person on earth, I'm not going to pass the time with him anymore. I'm not sitting next to him at school. I'm not sitting next to him on the bus. I'm not nodding to him on the street. He's not welcome in our home. If she catches me looking his way, she's going to beat the living daylights out of me because he's bad people.

Granpa T says J-Boy can't help it with his mama like she is.

Mama says that's one thing but her boy being friends with him is another thing and she is not going to have it. Her boy is going to stay off the streets. He's going to graduate from school. He's going to go on to college if he can. He's not going to run with the drugs and the guns and end up—and then she starts crying and Daddy says it's all right now. Li'l T is going to be just fine.

And then I say I can't stand J-Boy anyway and why would I want to run with him and ain't it about time for Baby Terrell to go to bed. And she wipes her face and says if I'm so worried about him getting to bed on time maybe I ought to clean up the kitchen so she can put him down. And I say, "Okay. I'll do it."

And finally everything's quiet.

I clean up, and then I go out and sit next to Buddy in the dark of the shed. He snugs up next to me. I bury my fingers in the fur behind his ears and I tickle the ends of that caterpillar eyebrow.

We sit still, listening to all the whispering nighttime

sounds. A pecan dropping on the shed roof. Somebody playing a radio down the street. Some lady calling her kids. The air conditioner kicking on. Something rustling in the pile of paint cans stacked up in the corner. When a car rolls by, we can feel the bass beating in the wood walls around us.

I hear Buddy breathing. I feel his soft fur and the muscles growing stronger and stronger under his skin. I hold my hand up to my face, and I smell his smell, and I think, *It's okay, Mama. It's all going to be just fine.*

16

I can't believe it when I look around and it's time for school to start up. Mama's going through all my school clothes and fussing about how they don't fit and what are we going to do. Daddy says we forgot about the glasses I'm supposed to get, and I promise to sit on the front row.

Tanya's sitting around with her thumb in her mouth because she's starting kindergarten for the first time and she's scared.

"It'll be okay," I tell her. "Just don't sing unless everybody else does."

Daddy takes me aside the last Saturday of the summer and he says, "How much you got saved, son?"

I say, "I've been spending my money on Buddy."

"You ain't spent it all on that dog, have you?"

"I've got fifty dollars," I say.

Daddy nods his head real slow. "That ain't much," he says.

"I know."

"But it might be just enough if I pitch in half," he says. Then he smiles. "Come on. Let's go shopping."

I can't believe it. Daddy takes me to the secondhand store down on Esplanade and the lady there says they got a whole stack of bikes in the back. We go back there and they've got red ones and blue ones and purple ones and orange ones.

Daddy makes me ride them around to try them out. "Which one fits you best?" he asks, and I say, "The red one."

We push it up to the front and the lady says, "That'll be eighty dollars on the nose."

Daddy slides two twenties on the counter, and so do I.

She starts counting it out, and Daddy says, "You're sure that bike is exactly eighty dollars? He's been mowing lawns all summer to get that money."

The lady looks at me. "What section did you take that bike out of?" she says.

"The very end," I say.

"Why you didn't say so to start?" she says. "That's the sale section. Those bikes are only sixty dollars." And then she gives me back a twenty.

We're putting that bike in the car and Daddy's tee-heeing and I'm grinning so big I think my face is going to split open.

"Sale section," Daddy says. "What do you think about that!"

•◆•

When we get home, all you-know-what's broke loose.

Baby Terrell's bawling and he's bleeding. Mama's screaming. Tanya's crying. Granpa T's yelling.

Daddy jumps out of the car. He goes running up the steps.

"That dog!" Mama's screaming.

She's holding Baby Terrell and looking at where he's bleeding on his forehead and on his foot. "That dog!" she screams again.

"What about the dog?" Daddy says.

"He bit the baby," Granpa T says.

I stop right where I am, pushing my new bike through the gate.

"Buddy bit Baby Terrell?" I say.

"Sorry, son," Granpa T says. "We can't have that."

"What do you mean?" I drop the bike and run back to the shed.

The door's shut and somebody's nailed Buddy's sign board across it. I hear Buddy inside, whimpering and crying.

"Buddy," I say through the door, "what happened? What happened, boy?"

Then Daddy's calling from the house. "Come in here, Li'l T," he's saying.

I go inside. Mama's washing Baby Terrell off in the sink. He's covered in dirt and blood. She's hugging him up every once in a while and kissing the top of his head.

"What happened?" I ask again.

"The dog bit the baby," Daddy says.

"He's out of here," Mama says. "He's gone tonight. I don't care where you take that dog. I don't care what you do with him. Shoot him. You hear what I'm saying? Get the gun out from under the mattress and shoot his brains out!"

Daddy puts his hand on Mama's arm. "Take it easy, now," he says.

"I say shoot him!" she says again, and I see she's got big old tears rolling down her cheeks. She's got dirt and blood smeared all across her apron.

Tanya's sitting on the floor in the corner, crying and sticking her thumb in her mouth. She's got on one of Mama's aprons and red shoes with glitter all over them.

"Just shoot him," Mama's saying over and over.

Then all a sudden, Tanya stands up and yells like she's in a whole different room, "But—it—ain't—his—fault!"

Everybody stops. Everybody looks at Tanya.

"What are you saying?" Granpa T says.

Tanya flops back down on the floor and sticks her thumb in her mouth and cries so hard her whole body's jerking around.

"What are you saying, baby girl?" Daddy says.

She takes her thumb out and looks up at Daddy and says, "You can't shoot him. You can't shoot Buddy."

"He bit the baby—"

"Baby Terrell was about to stick his hand in a rat's nest!" Tanya yells with her eyes all squinched up. "And Buddy stopped him."

Mama spins around like she's on the dance floor. Water goes flying across the kitchen. "What did you say?"

"We were playing with Buddy in the shed." Tanya's talking fast as she can. "I was singing and Baby Terrell was making a pie with the dirt. I gave him Buddy's bowl and he started spooning dirt into it. Buddy came over to see what was happening with his bowl. Baby Terrell took his spoon and whopped Buddy on the head. Buddy went 'Elp!' and slid back away. Baby Terrell laughed and crawled after Buddy and whopped him again and Buddy said 'Elp!' again and stood up and headed toward the door."

Tanya stops long enough to suck in three big breaths, then

she starts up again. "Baby Terrell went crawling across the floor toward Buddy. He was crawling past the paint cans. He saw something, and he stopped, and he crawled over and started to climb up. He was reaching. And then Buddy came barking back into the shed. He grabbed Baby Terrell's foot and he pulled him off the cans and Baby Terrell fell and hit his head and he started screaming and—"

She just stops. Her eyes stay squinched up.

"There's a rat's nest out there?" Daddy says to me.

"I heard something," I say.

"I saw them," Tanya says, and her eyes pop open. "When Baby Terrell fell he knocked the paint cans down and two big old rats went racing across the floor right in front of me and under the wall. And Buddy was limping after them and barking up a storm, and Baby Terrell was bleeding and—"

Then Tanya starts crying again and shaking and laying on the floor. Those red shoes are falling off her feet.

Mama looks at Tanya. Daddy looks at Mama. Granpa T looks at Daddy.

"Why didn't you tell me that to start?" Mama says.

Tanya don't answer. She curls up in a ball and starts hiccupping.

"Why were you just yelling, 'He bit the baby! He bit the baby!'?"

Baby Terrell's sitting in the sink splashing in the water. Granpa T walks over and takes him out.

"He needs a diaper," Mama says.

"I reckon I know that," Granpa T says, and walks out carrying the baby and talking in his ear. Baby Terrell starts laughing.

Mama looks at Daddy. Then she looks at me. "I changed my mind," she says. "Don't shoot him."

Then she rips off her apron, stomps up the stairs, and slams the door to her room.

Tanya sits up. She's hiccupping so hard she can't hardly slip her shoes back on.

"What were you doing all that time?" Daddy says. "Singing?"

Tanya covers her face with her hands.

"You were just watching and making up a song about what you were seeing, weren't you?"

Tanya presses her fingers against her eyes.

"And when it didn't work out, you blamed Buddy?" Daddy says.

Tanya almost nods.

"That ain't right," Daddy says.

"Don't hit her with the stick," I say. "She's too little."

Daddy looks at me a second, then he says, "I guess I'll

go take that board off the door. Ain't no use in keeping him penned up. We'll get the rats tomorrow."

When he leaves out, I sit down beside Tanya on the kitchen floor.

"I'm glad you told the truth," I say.

We're listening to Daddy's hammer prying off that old board and Buddy barking and barking. Tanya's sniffing and rubbing her nose like she wants to rub it off.

"You want to see my new bike?" I say.

"Can I ride it?"

"You ain't big enough," I say.

She follows me out to the front yard, and I pick up the bike where I dropped it. We're standing there looking at the red bike when Buddy comes limping around from the back. He comes up and sniffs me and pokes his nose in my hand. Then he goes to sniff Tanya.

"I'm sorry, Buddy," she says. "I know you're Li'l T's dog, but I love you, too."

He bends down and licks those red shoes on her feet, and all a sudden I'm wondering if Buddy loves her back.

17

I wish it wouldn't happen but it always does. No matter what, along comes August and off we go to school. I don't see J-Boy anywhere, so I don't have to worry about him anymore. Now it's that boy Rusty sitting next to me instead. I tell him I have a dog, and he says he wishes he had one, and I say why don't you come by my house someday and see mine, and he says okay. I ask him does he like to draw, and he shrugs his shoulders and says maybe.

We've been in school only a week when Daddy comes home from work Saturday evening and Granpa T meets him on the steps.

"Did you hear about this storm?" Granpa T says.

"What kind of storm?" Daddy says.

"It's a hurricane," Granpa T says. "They call it Katrina. They say it's a bad one."

"They're all bad," Daddy says.

"The mayor says we ought to leave," Granpa T says.

"He always says that," Daddy says. "Remember last time?"

Last time we didn't have Baby Terrell yet. He was still just a big old bump in Mama's stomach. Last time when the mayor said, "Get out of town," we all piled in the car and drove to Mississippi where Granpa T's people stay. Aunt Joyce, Granpa T's niece, let us stay in the spare room in her house. Mama and Daddy, me and Tanya, and Granpa T—all in the same room. We were all sound asleep when Mama started moaning in the middle of the night. Daddy said, "Oh, Lord," and pretty soon the whole house was awake except Granpa T and he was doing his going away trick that ain't really sleeping.

By morning we had a baby brother and the storm was somewhere in north Alabama. Daddy said we got to go home because he's got to work and I got to go to school. So we left Mama and Tanya and the baby in Mississippi with Aunt Joyce and got on the road with everybody in the whole city of New Orleans trying to get back. The sky was bluer than I'd ever seen and the sun was so hot I thought it was going to make the paint curl up off the roof of the car.

"I remember last time," Granpa T says, "and all I can say is, thank the Lord she ain't pregnant again."

"I mean the way everybody got all excited," Daddy says, "and then nothing happened. Those storms don't hit New Orleans. They always turn at the end."

"Don't let the devil hear you say that," Granpa T says, and he goes inside.

•◆•

Sunday morning we go to church and the preacher looks at me and says, "I heard about what that dog did."

I say, "He's a good dog, Brother James. He takes care of things. He's walking real good now. He even climbs up a few steps. I'm going to make him a pirate leg and he'll do even better."

"You're the instrument of God," Brother James says. "God was waiting for your car so that dog could have a happy life."

"With only three legs?" I say.

"There's always a price," Brother James says, and shakes his head. "Happiness always comes with a price."

When he calls us to prayer, he talks about Buddy. He talks about how everybody came together and saved God's creature and how helping each other is what God meant us to do.

And then he starts praying louder. He raises up his voice and he says, "A storm is coming, Lord. A storm is coming."

At first I think he's talking about evil as usual, but this time he's talking about rain and wind.

"The mayor came on the TV this morning," Brother James prays. "He came on the TV and he said, 'You got to leave.' He said it's mandatory. And, Lord, what does mandatory mean? It means you got to. Lord, we got to leave our homes.

"Lord, there's some of us who have a way. We've got cars or we've got people who've got cars. Lord, give us the strength to gather our families and put them in the cars and take them to safety.

"But, Lord, there's some of us who don't have a way. Some of us are too old and some of us are too young and some of us are too poor. Lord, help us to reach out to our brothers and sisters who don't have a way. Help us to put them in our cars with us. Help us to take them to the Superdome if they need a ride. Help us, Lord, to help each other—just like we helped old Buddy—so we can gather together again next Sunday and raise our voices in praise and joy just like we're doing today. Hallelujah!"

And the choir starts singing, and Mama casts her eye

on Daddy and Daddy looks back at her and raises up his eyebrows, and I know we're leaving again.

•◆•

Mama starts packing the minute we get home. She starts with Baby Terrell's stuff. She pulls out all his diapers and bottles and toys and stroller and port-a-crib, and then Daddy says, "We can't take all that, woman." And Mama makes a face like she's sucking a lemon but she puts back the toys and the stroller and the port-a-crib.

"Who're we going to take with us?" I say to her. "Like Brother James says?"

Mama stops stuffing a bag and looks at me. "You haven't got the sense you were born with, boy. Where are we going to put somebody else? Tie them on the roof?" She shakes her head and snatches up Baby Terrell right before he pulls over the lamp. "Go get a suitcase," she says. "Pack two nights of clothes. Help Tanya pack, too."

Daddy's in the kitchen filling up a cooler and Granpa T's shifting around in his room putting things in a paper sack.

"Maybe we ought to take Mrs. Washington to the Superdome," I say to him.

"We'd have to drag her out," Granpa T says. "And

anyway, how's she going to make do with all those strangers and she's half blind?"

He sets his sack on the table and I look inside. There's a box of pictures, his Bible, his pills, and two pair of undershorts.

"You're packing light," I say.

"We ain't going to be gone long."

Tanya's sitting on the sofa with her doll, about to cry.

"Do what your mama told you to do," Granpa T says. "Go help your sister pack."

So I drag Tanya upstairs and make her pick out some clothes. We're fighting about whether she can pack her ballerina skirt and those red shoes when I hear Daddy calling me.

"Li'l T," he's yelling. "Go get Buddy and bring him inside."

I go running down the stairs. "Why inside?" I say.

"Can't leave him outside," Daddy says.

"Leave?" I say.

"We can't take Buddy with us," Daddy says. "There ain't room in the car."

All a sudden, I can't move. I'm standing there like a statue. My fingertips are throbbing and my feet feel like rocks.

"Then I won't go," I say.

Daddy stops still and stares at me.

"I'll stay here with Buddy. I'll look after the house. Y'all won't be gone long. Maybe I'll go stay with Mrs. Washington."

"I said bring Buddy inside." Daddy's looking at me like he's one inch away from getting that stick up by the shed. "Now," he says, and turns around and walks off.

I go outside and Buddy's laying on his blanket. He lifts up his nose when he sees me, and his tail goes *thump*. I sit down and rest my elbows on my knees. Then I bend down my head and hold it in my two hands.

I ain't touching Buddy or even looking at him. But I can feel him. It's like the whole shed is filled up with him being there. He moves his feet and his claws scratch a little on the floor. His tail thumps against the wall. I hear him breathing—not panting but not real quiet either. I know the tip of his tongue is hanging out the side of his mouth. I know his whole body is moving just the slightest bit with each breath. Then I hear his teeth click together when he closes his mouth and the rustle of the blanket as he lays his head down. I know he's looking at me with his big, soft eyes just like he always does.

I can't leave Buddy.

I can't not leave Buddy.

I lift up my head and see his eyes turned up to look at me.

He waits a second then he gets up and limps over to where I'm sitting. He pokes his nose at my hand where it's holding up my head. He licks my ear.

I know they're all running around like crazy inside. I know I could just walk out the gate and Buddy would follow me and they wouldn't ever see. I could go wherever I wanted. We could find a shed somewhere and hide. I'd take his blanket and at night we'd sleep on it together. When I was sure everybody was gone, we'd sneak back. His food and his bowls would be waiting. I'd break in the house and make soup. Once the storm passed, I'd check on Mrs. Washington and make sure she was okay. I'd bring her some of the soup. Buddy would lay on her front porch and we'd sit in her swing and she'd give me a cold drink and I'd read her letters to her and maybe I'd cut her grass for free. When I came back home, I'd go up on the roof and fix the hole where a pecan branch broke off in the storm.

Now Buddy's licking my cheek like it's a Popsicle. I take his face in my hands and he licks my whole face.

When they got home, the house would be fixed and Mrs. Washington would be safe and they'd say—

All a sudden Granpa T shows up at the door. "You coming, son?" he says.

"I can't leave Buddy," I say, and a little hiccup comes out.

Granpa T sits down beside me. "Why do you love that ugly, old dog so much?"

"I just do."

"I loved my chicken." Granpa T's rubbing my back. "Can you imagine that? Loving a chicken?"

I don't say nothing.

Granpa T stands up. "You ain't got no choice, son," he says. "I'll carry the dog food."

He grabs up the bag and heads toward the house. I don't move. He turns around. "We're all waiting," he says, and goes on inside.

I stand up and lead Buddy out of the shed. He's following me, but his tail ain't wagging.

"Two days," I'm telling him. "It's only two days."

He stops still at the bottom of the steps.

"You can do it," I say. "You're strong enough."

He hops up the steps one at a time. I hold the door open for him. It's the first time he's ever been inside. He bends down and starts sniffing at the rug like he ain't sure this is where he's supposed to be.

"I don't like a dog in my house," Mama says.

"It ain't your house," Granpa T says.

"We're putting him in the big bathroom upstairs," Daddy says. "We'll shut him up."

It's hard for Buddy to make it up the stairs. Finally, Daddy reaches down and picks him up. "He's a lot heavier," Daddy says. "You're feeding him too much."

We're all standing in the bathroom. Buddy's walking around, sniffing at the corners and poking his nose at the trash can. Granpa T's running a bathtub full of water. Daddy's setting up the food bag in the corner and cutting a hole in the bottom so Buddy can eat straight out the bag.

"Where is he going to pee, Daddy?" I say. "Where is he going to do his business?"

"He'll figure it out," Daddy says.

Then Buddy starts kind of running around the bathroom in little circles. He's making whimpery sounds. His tail's going down between his hind legs. He knows we're leaving him. He knows what it feels like.

Granpa T turns off the water and Buddy runs over and licks out a little. He's got enough water to last forever it looks like. He runs over and takes a bite of his food. He comes over and pokes his nose at my hand. His big old brown eyes are looking up at me like he's wondering if this is for true, like he can't believe I'd do this to him.

I start toward the door and he's right beside me. He's glued up so close I'm almost tripping on him.

"Make him stay," Daddy says.

I walk to the back of the bathroom and Buddy walks with me.

"Sit, Buddy," I say, and he sits.

"Stay," I say, and start backing up toward the door. All a sudden, Daddy grabs my arm and snatches me out the room. Daddy slams the door and we hear Buddy running across the tile. Then we hear him scratching on the door.

"You're going to have to paint that door when we get back," Daddy says.

Then Buddy starts to howl. I ain't never heard that sound before.

"Arroooo!" Buddy's crying. "Arrooo!"

I put my hand on the door and feel it shaking.

"Buddy," I say, but he just keeps on, wailing and moaning like he ain't never heard me. Like he ain't never even known me.

I'm standing there and something big's trying to go down my throat. I'm feeling my eyes get stingy, and Buddy keeps on howling.

"Two days?" I say to Daddy.

"Two days," Daddy says.

18

It usually takes an hour and a half to get to Aunt Joyce's place in Mississippi. This time it takes eight. We're sitting on the superhighway with everybody and his brother. The cars are backed up along the road as far as you can see, all shining in the hot sun.

When we're on the bridge crossing Lake Pontchartrain, some cars start driving down the shoulder lane, and Daddy starts cussing.

Mama says, "T Junior, that doesn't help," and he shuts up.

It takes us four hours just to get from our house to the other side of that bridge. Once we get across the lake, I see a man get out of the passenger door of a car and walk along the side of the road for a while. He bends down, touches his toes a few times, and does some jumping jacks. Then he turns around and goes back to his car. Traffic is moving that slow.

Baby Terrell starts up fussing and Granpa T's got his head tilted back as usual. Tanya's singing to herself in the backseat. After a while, Mama starts up some hymns. I wish I had my Game Boy back.

Eight hours is a long time to sit in a car that ain't hardly moving.

We make Aunt Joyce's house long after dark. She's got a whole plate of fried chicken waiting and a big old pot of gumbo. We eat and we talk. I tell Aunt Joyce all about Buddy. She says she had a dog once. She named him Spot because he had a white circle around one eye. He had four legs but lost part of his ear in a fight. Aunt Joyce can't remember what became of Spot. She says she'd have to ask her mama and her mama's passed.

Daddy and Granpa T sit out on the front porch and drink their beer. They don't have any neighbors to talk to because we're so far out in the country. There ain't no other houses. There ain't no cars. There ain't no lights.

Tanya's running around in the dark trying to catch fireflies while Aunt Joyce looks for a jar. Mama's sitting on the swing holding Baby Terrell and humming.

I walk out into the open yard where Aunt Joyce has a little garden growing tomatoes. At home you have to lift the tomatoes up to your nose and give them a good sniff if you want to smell them. Here they soak up the sun all day and then sit there in the dark, sending off their tomato smell to everybody in the yard. I get myself a good noseful and then walk farther out under the trees.

Aunt Joyce must have fifty trees in her yard. They're tall, tall pine trees. I got to bend my head way back to see the needles all at the top. The wind is moving them just the tiniest bit and they're making a quiet *whush-whush*ing sound. I can see lots of stars through the trees, but I can see the clouds are starting to blow in, too.

When I get back to the porch, Daddy and Granpa T are looking up. They're feeling the air.

"It's coming," Granpa T says.

"I'll be glad when it's gone," Mama says. "I already want to lie down in my own bed."

I hear her voice in the dark and I think how quiet it is at home right now with everybody gone.

How quiet and dark.

I'm wondering what Buddy is thinking. I'm wondering if he's scared.

I wrinkle up my forehead and I squinch my eyes shut and I send him a message. *Two days, Buddy,* I think. *Just wait. Two days.*

•◆•

When I wake up Monday morning, I'm covered in sweat.

We're all sleeping in the same room again. Mama and Daddy are on the bed. Granpa T is on a sofa pushed against the wall. Baby Terrell's in a crib borrowed from the people down the road. Me and Tanya are rolled up in blankets on the floor.

The ceiling fan ain't moving and there ain't no air coming out the vents. The alarm clock is dead.

And the storm is on us.

I'm laying there, sweating and listening to the wind.

I ain't never heard wind like that before. It sounds like a ship on the river and a cat screaming and a whistle blowing all at the same time. And it don't stop. It just keeps going on and on and on.

The pipes in the walls are rattling and the glass in the windows is shaking. The curtains are blowing in and out even though the windows are locked shut. Every once in a while the rain slams against the windows like somebody threw a bucket of gravel straight at the glass.

I hear footsteps and it's Mama. She's tippy-toeing across the room. She pulls Baby Terrell out of the crib. He's so asleep he almost flops out of her arms. She takes him in the bed with her. I see her crawling under the covers and tucking Baby Terrell up between her and Daddy. I feel Tanya next to me. In the dark I can barely see her eyes shining at me, wide open and still. "Don't be scared," I whisper, and pull her closer.

Underneath all the sounds of the wind, there's a howling sound. A howling sound like Buddy's. I'm laying there with Tanya all snugged up next to me and I feel like I can hear him all the way in New Orleans. He's sitting on that cold floor. That old house is shaking, and he's hearing the wind just like I am. He's tilting his head back. His mouth is opening up. And out comes that sound. "You left me, Li'l T," he's saying, and all the sadness in his heart is just pouring out in that little, bitty bathroom all by himself.

I'm squinching up my eyes and trying to send him a message. "Be brave, Buddy," I'm saying. "Be brave."

And then all a sudden something outside explodes. Loud. Like a bomb's been dropped.

And again and again and again.

I hear Mama's voice praying. She's praying almost as loud as the wind but I can't make out her words.

And then Daddy's bending down beside us and saying,

"Everybody under the bed," and we're all crowding up under where it's dusty and there are probably spiders, but we ain't thinking about that.

Daddy's head is up beside me and I whisper in his ear, "What's that sound, Daddy?"

"The trees," Daddy says. "All those pine trees are popping in two."

We lay under the bed and listen.

One after the other the trees explode, and we hear the sound of the branches breaking as they crash past each other to the ground, and then they hit, and sometimes the whole house bounces and somewhere in the house we hear glass shatter, and always we hear that wind blowing and screaming and howling.

And now I'm thinking about the window in our bathroom and the pecan tree beside our house and my mind is so tight with pictures I can't send any more messages to Buddy.

We're laying there so long I forget there's any other place to be. I forget my name is Li'l T. It's almost like being asleep except it's completely different. I feel Daddy beside me. Sometimes he's stiff. Sometimes he's praying. When I remember, I say my prayers, too. And I cross my fingers just in case.

When it's finally quiet, we creep out from under the bed. Granpa T's so stiff he can't hardly move. Mama's got dust balls in her hair. Tanya's practically sucked her thumb off her hand, and Baby Terrell needs a new diaper bad.

We find Aunt Joyce locked in her bathroom. Daddy gets her to come out. All together we open the front door and look out into the drippy, morning sun.

All the pine trees in her yard are down. Every single one.

And the air smells sparkly and clean, like a Christmas tree lot.

The electricity pole is broke in two and half is laying on the ground. One little tree is leaning on the roof of the front porch. All the other trees between the house and the road are snapped and cracked and blocking the driveway. Our car is crushed and Aunt Joyce's car is penned in between two tree trunks twice as big around as a utility pole.

"We ain't going nowhere soon," Granpa T says.

Aunt Joyce bends down and picks up something laying on the front porch. It's a shingle. Then I see the yard is full of them. She sighs. "We don't have any electricity," she says. "Don't open the refrigerator unless you have to. We'll fire up the grill to cook. The rescue trucks'll come soon."

I look at Daddy. "You said two days."

He looks back at me. "What do you want me to do about it?" he says, and goes clomping out on the porch to sit.

19

Once the storm clears up, it gets hotter than ever. The air is still and quiet. There ain't no breeze blowing. There ain't no birds singing.

My guess is, there ain't no birds left and if there is, there ain't nowhere for them to sit. When we stand on the porch and look out, Aunt Joyce's yard looks like an ocean of pine branches with broke-off trunks sticking up every once in a while. Daddy asks Aunt Joyce if she's got a saw he can start cutting some of the branches with. He says he wants to cut a path to the garden. He wants to make his way to her car. She finds a half-rusted saw and an old ax in a closet by her washing machine. She says they ain't been used in a thousand years, and they look it.

Daddy picks them up, heads outside, and starts chopping.

Every morning Daddy and Granpa T sit in Aunt Joyce's car and listen to the radio. When I ask Daddy what he's listening to, he just looks at me and tells me to go pick up some shingles. I'm making a pile of shingles beside Daddy's pile of branches. I can't help but notice they ain't all the same kind of shingles and there ain't no other house nearby that I can see.

We eat steak and chicken from the freezer. We drink hot drinks out of the can. We run out of clean clothes. We pull all the tomatoes still hanging on the vines.

Mama says she's losing count of the days, but I ain't. Every night when I lay down on my pallet, I say to myself, "That's another one."

I lay there and I'm wondering where in that bathroom does Buddy lay himself down. That tile is cold and hard, and we didn't put his blanket in there with him. I'm wondering if he can eat all he needs out of that hole in the bag. I'm wondering what if the stopper don't work in the tub and all the water drains out.

Sometimes I think about the window and the pecan tree and I squinch up my eyes and I think as hard as I can to Buddy.

When I get home, I'm thinking to him, *I'm going to make it up to you. I promise.* I tell him I'll sell my bicycle back to the lady and it'll be dog biscuits every day. I tell him I'll make him that leg. I know Granpa T will help me. We'll walk to the river. *It won't be long, Buddy,* I'm thinking to him. *It won't be long.*

But no rescue trucks come.

We've been living in that house without electricity for five days.

On day six Mama says, "We got to get milk. This baby needs milk."

Granpa T nods real slow. "And I need my medicine."

"Are you about out?" Daddy says real sharp.

Granpa T pulls the little brown bottle out of his pocket and shakes it. It don't make hardly any noise.

"Why didn't you say something before?" Daddy asks, and then he looks at Aunt Joyce. "How far are we from town?"

"Ten miles," she says.

Daddy looks down at his shoes. "I can walk ten miles," he says, and heads for the door.

We run after him. "When will you be back, Daddy?"

"When I get back," he says.

We wait all day. We wait all night. We wait all morning.

Baby Terrell's crying something bad. Mosquitoes have bitten his arms all to pieces but we have to keep the windows open because it's so hot. Mama's run out of diapers and Aunt

Joyce is ripping up her sheets. Tanya's sucking on her thumb all day. Mama sits on the front porch and fans herself. Granpa T sits on the sofa and leans his head back. He hardly moves at all. He's gone and can't nobody go with him.

When it's almost night again, we hear a truck a long way off. We all jump up, and then after a while we see Daddy walking down the long drive with two other men. They got great big saws. They pull the cords and fire them up, and then they start cutting their way to the house. We can smell the pine trees again. We're jumping up and down and cheering. When they're done, me and Tanya go running down the road to Daddy and we jump in his arms. Mama's standing on the porch yelling, "Thank you! Thank you!"

Daddy grabs us up. He stinks something bad but it smells good. He sends us down the road. "Ride with the men," he says. "We'll be right behind you."

Mama and Aunt Joyce are already piling stuff in Aunt Joyce's car, and I'm thinking, *We're going home at last.* I'm thinking when I open that bathroom door Buddy's probably going to knock me over he'll be so glad to see me. I'm thinking I'll take him outside, and we'll walk a little in the yard to stretch his legs, and then I'll take him to the shed, and we'll sit in the dark, and I'll tell him about the storm, and he'll listen to every word. Every single word.

Get ready, Buddy, I'm thinking. *Here I come*.

"Are you taking us all the way to New Orleans?" I say to the men.

They laugh. "Just to town," they say.

All the way in, we're looking at what that storm did. Trees are down everywhere. Electricity lines are laying around like spaghetti. Some houses have their roofs torn off. One house has a swimming pool ripped up and laying against the front porch. Cars are laying around upside down and sideways. One store has its big, plate-glass window busted and yards of cloth trailing out into the parking lot.

"Is it like this in New Orleans?" I say.

They look at me. "You ain't heard?" they say.

"Heard what?" I say.

"New Orleans flooded," they say. "The levees broke. Everything is under water."

Tanya sucks in her breath.

I sit real quiet.

The engine is loud in that truck.

"Everything?" I say.

"Yessiree," one man says. "Right up to the rooftops. Everything. Ain't nothing living in that town no more."

The men take us to the shelter in town. It's a big arena where football teams play their games. Out front there's a long line of people waiting to get in. Some of them are carrying suitcases. Some have garbage bags. Most of them don't have anything at all.

The men wait with us until the others get there, then they're gone.

Daddy says they're headed out to find other people stuck in their houses in the country. He says he already helped them cut the trees to two other houses today. He says at one house, the lady was dead and the man didn't want to leave. "They're too old for this," Daddy says. "We had to carry the man out the door. He was crying like a baby the whole way."

Aunt Joyce takes one look at that line of people waiting to get in the shelter and she says there ain't no way she going to stay in a shelter. She says she's driving up to Atlanta right now to stay with her daughter even if she has to drive all night. She tells Granpa T to come on with her, but he says no. She begs him and begs him, but he keeps shaking his head. Finally she says there ain't no fool like an old fool and drives off, leaving us waiting in line with everybody else. When we get to the front they give us badges to wear. They write down numbers off Daddy's driver's license. They take us to six cots lined up in a row on about the fifty-yard line. "How's Baby Terrell going to sleep on a cot?" Mama says. Daddy puts his hand on her arm and says, "We're the lucky ones."

I'm sitting there on my folding cot. Granpa T's shaking his head. Mama's opening the milk the ladies gave us. Tanya's sucking her thumb.

I can't help it. I blurt it right out.

"The men in the truck told us New Orleans is flooded. They said everything is under water. Everything."

Mama's busy with the baby. Granpa T's looking around for the shelter doctor. They don't look at me.

But Daddy looks at me. He looks at me a long time.

"It's true, son," he finally says. "Everything."

He looks at me a little while longer. "I'm sorry," he says. "I'm real, real sorry."

I lay down on my cot. I curl up. I close my eyes. I go to a place where nobody else can go. Not even Granpa T.

20

We ain't got nowhere to live now so we stay in that shelter. There must be about a million other people living there with us, all in the same room. Half the people are from Mississippi. They're telling about a giant wave that washed everything away—streets, houses, apartment buildings. I can't hardly believe it but they're telling about it on TV, too. The other half of the people are from New Orleans. I lay there on my cot and I think about what if I see somebody I know. What if my teacher walks down the aisle? Or that boy Rusty? What if I see the lady who cuts Mama's hair or Mr. Nelson with the truck or Mrs. Washington? What if I see J-Boy walking by with his mama following behind him in her nightgown? I think about that and I look at all the faces, but I don't see nobody I know. All those faces and not a single one of them is somebody I've ever seen before.

Every day different workers come in and talk to the people. They're trying to get us clothes and toothbrushes. They're trying to feed us and find us places to live. They're trying to match up families.

People make signs and go walking up and down the aisles between the cots. The signs are just lists of names—all the people they can't find. One lady says the names are her children. She says she was visiting her mama in the hospital in Jackson when the storm came. The neighbor was watching her babies. She calls and calls but the phones don't work. Now she don't know where any of them are. She's riding from shelter to shelter carrying her sign. Every day she walks the aisles someplace else.

I wonder if anybody is looking for us. I wonder if the news is telling about the storm all the way up in Chicago. I wonder if anybody tried to call us. I wonder what would happen if somebody wrote us a letter. Where would it go?

The shelter's getting fuller and fuller. We squeeze the cots closer together. They make rules about who uses the bathroom when.

"You should have gone with Joyce," Daddy tells Granpa T. "I'll bet she would come back and get you if we called her."

"What am I going to do sleeping on the sofa in her daughter's apartment in Atlanta?" Granpa T says.

Daddy shrugs up his shoulders and Granpa T lays back down on his cot. He closes his eyes and goes to sleep—or wherever.

Because to tell the truth, can't nobody really sleep in that shelter with all those people always moving and talking. All day long they're talking loud. All night long they're whispering. They're tossing and turning. They're going to the bathroom. The babies are crying. And when it's just barely light, the loud talking starts up again. "Move over." "Where you from?" "How much water did you get?"

And one thing everybody's talking about is what it looks like in New Orleans. You can't get away from it. They're saying how the only thing you can see is the roofs of the houses. For miles and miles there ain't nothing but black water and roofs. How the helicopters come and take the people off their roofs. How they've got boats everywhere pulling people out of the water. How they've got bodies floating around and tangled up in the trees and putrefying in the houses where they were trapped when the water rushed up.

They've got the TV going all the time. They're showing pictures of the buildings burning, right in the middle of the water. Can't nobody get close enough to help, and the buildings just keep on burning.

I'm watching that news and I'm thinking that can't be real. That can't be my home. That's got to be a movie. And then I see I'm sitting on a cot in a shelter in Mississippi.

One day they show a dog swimming through the water. He's black and his tail is sticking out straight behind him. I jump up off my cot and run over to take a look. He's making a V-shaped ripple through the water and he's barely able to keep his head up. The rescuers are standing in a boat and wearing yellow vests with orange belts. They're saying, "Come on, boy! You can do it!" And they're reaching out to him and grabbing him and dragging him up into that boat. That dog shakes water all over the place. The rescuers hold their hands up to protect their faces and you can see they're smiling and I've got my face right up to that TV.

But when the rescuers step back and the dog stands still, I can see he ain't got no caterpillar eyebrow. His throat ain't white underneath. He's got all four of his legs.

I lay back down on my cot. What am I doing thinking that dog might be Buddy? Even if he got out, even if he struggled through the window, even if he heard me calling and calling him in my sleep, how's he going to swim with only three legs? What's a dog like Buddy going to do in a world filled up with water?

One shelter lady gives me a Game Boy. I sit on my cot and play it every day. I don't do nothing else. I don't talk. I don't eat except when I have to. Mama keeps saying, "Are you okay, son?" and I don't answer. Baby Terrell starts walking in that shelter and Mama has to chase after him. Tanya makes friends with two girls with cots near hers. They fix each other's hair. Tanya looks pretty stupid afterward but she's happy.

A lady two cots over starts having a baby. They whisk her off while her fiancé is in the bathroom and he don't have any idea where they took her. He sits there crying until somebody comes and leads him away by the hand. One old man stands up on the far end of the room and starts trying to take off all his clothes. His wife is screaming at him and he's saying he's itching all over. Granpa T sits up and watches that show awhile. When the lady finally makes the man stop, Granpa T lays back down and closes his eyes.

I go to the next level.

•◆•

We've been in that shelter almost a week when Daddy comes up to Granpa T and says, "Wake up. I've got something to tell you."

Granpa T opens his eyes. "I ain't asleep," he says.

"They told me it ain't all flooded," Daddy says. "They told me around our street, there are places where the water ain't so deep. Some places."

Granpa T raises up on his elbows.

"One man here told me he's driving down tomorrow morning just to look," Daddy says. "He wants to see how much water he got in his house."

Granpa T shakes his head. "Too much," he says.

Daddy don't listen to him. "He can't stay, of course. There ain't nowhere to stay."

Daddy crosses his arms over his chest and looks at Mama sitting on the cot behind me. "He asked me to ride with him," Daddy says. "And I'm going."

Granpa T sits up. I put down the Game Boy.

"I want to know if you want to come," Daddy says to Granpa T. "There's room."

Granpa T shakes his head. "You go first," he says. "I ain't ready." Then he lays back down and closes his eyes.

I open my mouth and out come the first words I've said in almost a week. "Can I come?" I say it real quick, and then I shut up.

Daddy looks hard at me. Mama stands up behind me.

"It ain't going to be easy," Daddy says. "We won't get back here until late."

"I can do it," I say, and push the Game Boy off to one side.

Daddy looks up at Mama. I know she's shaking her head. I know her mouth's making the shape of "No." Daddy looks down at me again.

"You're old enough," he says. "You can come."

•◆•

We get in the man's truck before light. I'm sitting between him and Daddy. They're drinking coffee. We're riding with the windows open. The cool of the morning is coming in with the smell of all the pine trees. We're going along looking at the white, broke trunks pointing up to the sky. Behind us, the sun starts to come up. We have to go around the lake to get into town. That storm washed the bridge to pieces. The concrete slabs of that superhighway bridge just floated off like toy boats. Daddy says they've got real boats stacked up in the marshes like dead fish. He says they've got boats sitting on top of bridges down by Empire. He says they've got barges sitting on top of houses in the Lower Ninth Ward.

That's a lot of water, I'm thinking. That's enough water to fill up a city. That's enough water to fill up a house.

We're taking the back roads. The man tells us they got the army blocking the main ways. They got piles of dirt and gravel dumped across the roads so nobody can get through.

They got soldiers standing there with guns, and they won't let you pass. He tells us they got people tearing up the city. They're breaking down the windows and stealing everything they can lay their hands on. He says the mayor don't want nobody coming into town. They're afraid people from the country going to come and join up with the thugs. They're afraid it's going to get out of hand.

Daddy says, "It's already out of hand."

"That's so," says the man. "That's truly so."

•◆•

When we get into the city, the man stays close to the river, where the land is higher and there ain't no flooding. But everywhere we look, trees are broke or fallen down. It's just like Mississippi except these are oak trees. On some of them, the root balls are sticking up almost as high as a house. The trees pulled up sidewalks and fences and even houses when they fell over. All the yards are full up with broke limbs and trash. They got pieces of fence and strips of tin roof laying on the street. They got patio chairs sitting in the branches of the trees that are still standing up. They got a mattress twisted up in some wires hanging off a pole.

We're driving over electricity lines and phone lines draping all over the streets. We're crunching branches and trash. Everywhere you turn there are great big old potholes that could swallow your car. Daddy says to the man driving, "Watch out," and the man swerves that truck one way, then another.

And this ain't even where the water is. This ain't even the part we've been seeing on TV.

It takes us almost an hour just to get to our neighborhood. The man lets us down near our church. That church is standing there all high and dry. It ain't flooded at all and the grass needs cutting. The front door is wide open. Daddy walks up the steps. Inside it's cooler. He shouts out, "Hello!"

A man stands up behind the altar. It's Brother James.

"Praise God," Brother James says. "It's you."

He and Daddy are standing there hugging like they're real brothers. Then Brother James turns and hugs me. He's sweaty like he ain't bathed in days.

"Your family?" he says to Daddy.

"Safe," Daddy says. "We went to my cousin's place in Mississippi. After the storm, she went on up to her daughter's place in Atlanta. Now we're in a shelter."

"Praise God," Brother James says again.

Daddy sort of waves his hand around at the chairs standing in the church.

"Everybody?" he says.

"Mrs. Washington passed," Brother James says. "She drowned in her attic."

Daddy covers his eyes with his hand.

"Brother Thomas is in the hospital in Houston. His heart went bad on him. And those Cary boys have been pulling people out. They got their fishing boat and they've been going back and forth." He stops for a minute and looks out the window. "But they've left now. They're worn out."

Daddy finishes rubbing his eyes and nods. "We're going to the house," he says.

"You can't get there," Brother James says.

Daddy looks at him.

"Your street's flooded up to the eaves. Twelve feet of water at least. I'm sorry, T Junior. You're going to have to tell your daddy about his house. Y'all ain't got nothing left. It's all gone. Everything."

"But what about Buddy?" I say.

"Buddy?" Brother James says.

"We left him locked in the bathroom. The car was too little for him to fit. He's been waiting and waiting."

Brother James looks at Daddy. "You were planning on getting that dog?"

Daddy nods.

"You can't get there, son," Brother James says. "Your house is standing in the middle of a lake."

"But I can swim. I know how."

"You can't swim in that black water. You don't even know what's in there. And what's your family going to do if you drown yourself going after that dog? Buddy was a street dog when you found him. Now he's got to take care of his own self again."

"But he's only got three legs now."

Brother James stoops down and looks me in the eye. "You can't get to that dog, Li'l T. It's the Lord's will," he says. "And there ain't nothing you can do about it."

21

The next day, I just lay there on my cot. Some boys in the shelter are starting to make gangs. They're coming up to people and acting big. The boss of the shelter takes them and puts them in a room with a counselor.

I'm thinking about what that would be like, sitting in a room with this white lady saying, "What's troubling you now?"

And I think, *What do you say first?* The bathrooms in this shelter stink. I can't eat watery red beans and rice one more time. I want my own clothes, not these ones with somebody else's name written in the neck. I want to watch the TV shows I like. I want a place where I can be by myself.

I want my dog.

I'm laying there and I close my eyes and I go flying. I go

right out the window and over the broke pine trees and all that black water and I land right on the roof of our house. I lean over the edge and I look at the bathroom window.

Is that window covered up with water? Is it high and dry? Is it broke open? Is Buddy gone, roaming the streets and looking for food? Is he sitting there in the corner, panting in the heat and cocking up his eyebrow, just waiting for me to come let him loose? Or is he—?

And that's where the flying stops. I can't see nothing else.

Daddy's gone almost all day. When he shows up that evening, I'm still laying on my cot playing my Game Boy and Granpa T is laying on his cot looking at his pictures.

"What are you looking at?" Daddy says to Granpa T.

"Your mama," Granpa T says, and hands one of the pictures to Daddy. "She's been gone a long time," he says, "but I'll be seeing her again soon."

"What are you talking about? You've got a long time yet," Daddy says. "It's going to be all right now. We're leaving this shelter. I've got a job."

Mama sings out, "Praise the Lord!"

Granpa T sits up. "Where are you working?"

Daddy says, "Right here in town. I'm going to help them clear up all these trees. Going to work with the same crew I helped before."

"But where are we going to live?" Mama says.

"The church will give us a place to start," Daddy says, "and it's all furnished. We get three months free, then we pay rent."

"Hallelujah," Mama says. "Praise God."

Daddy looks down at me. "And the kids are going back to school again. Right here in town."

"But when are we moving back to New Orleans?" I say.

"I hope never," Mama says. "Next time I see that place will be too soon for me."

"I want to go home," I say.

"This is home now," Daddy says. "We're starting over."

•◆•

They put us up in an apartment building on the other side of town. Stacked up on top of ours are maybe three more apartments, and they each have a balcony stuck on the front. We've got a little square of grass that I could cut in five minutes with a pair of scissors. Right in front of our grass is the parking lot. And then there's a six-lane highway with cars blasting back and forth all day long and making a circle all the way around the whole town.

Everywhere you look there's plenty of cars, cement, and buildings. But one thing there ain't hardly any of is trees.

There weren't too many to start with and whatever there was got broke off in the storm. There ain't no iron fences neither. And there ain't no front porches or steps to sit on. There ain't no corner to the street, and as far as I can see, there ain't no end to it neither.

Tanya's standing out front clapping her hands and pointing at the raggedy flower boxes hanging on the front windows of every first-floor apartment. Baby Terrell is trying to walk up the sidewalk to the wrong apartment. Mama's saying how are we going to remember which one is ours. Granpa T's saying he thinks we're up to it.

Then Daddy puts the key in the door and in we go.

That apartment ain't hardly as big as the first floor of our house in New Orleans. It's mostly one big room with the kitchen and the table and the TV, and then off to the side are two little bedrooms. Granpa T stretches out on the sofa and says he guesses he'll sleep there because that's where he spends most of his time anyway.

Mama and Daddy take the bedroom that has a big bed, a crib, and a bureau with four drawers. Daddy opens those drawers and laughs and says all he needs now is some clothes, and Mama says he better not get too many because that's where she plans to put hers.

The other bedroom has two twin beds so close together

you almost have to turn sideways to get between them. Mama says me and Tanya get that room and we have to make up our minds which bed is whose.

"Which one you want?" I say to Tanya.

She's standing there looking and looking, trying to decide.

I push past her. "I pick this one," I say, and lay down on the one farthest from the door.

"But I want that one."

"Too late," I say. I turn over and stare at the wall.

The next morning, Daddy starts his job, and Mama takes us down to the school office. They give us uniforms for the school. They've got a whole big room set up with cafeteria tables loaded down with red and white shirts and khaki shorts and skirts. They've got piles of belts in one corner and a whole stack of book bags in another.

When we walk in, the ladies are all smiles. They say how they are so glad we can come to their school. They say how all the families gave their old uniforms so the Katrina kids can come to school. They tell Mama one store in town gave away all these book bags. They give her a piece of paper to take to some other place where somebody else is giving out free paper and pencils.

They're patting us on the back and holding shirts up

against my chest. They're saying what a strong-looking boy I am. They're saying how Tanya is cute as a button. Tanya's showing all her teeth in her grin and I'm thinking I'm tireder than I've ever been in my whole life. I'm thinking I just want to go back to that apartment and climb in my bed and go to sleep.

That night Daddy is worn out at supper. He's saying he's awful out of shape but he'll get stronger. Mama's saying she made his favorite roast. Granpa T's saying he thinks he can fix up the apartment so the doors don't squeak if somebody would buy a little can of WD-40. Tanya's saying her doll likes the new bed. Baby Terrell is sitting in the high chair somebody gave us and rubbing his hands in his peas. After looking at that, I'm thinking I don't even want to eat. I just want to go to bed.

I'm still tired the next morning when I head off to school. My teacher's name is Mrs. Watson. She looks like she's about six feet tall. She's got red hair hanging down to her shoulders. She's wearing a blue dress. I walk in the door and she looks up and she says, "Ah! Tyrone. Welcome."

And I think to myself, *I ain't Tyrone.*

She shows me where to hang up my bag. She hands me a stack of books. She shows me a desk. It has my name written on a card taped right on the tabletop. I sit down. I look around. Everybody's busy doing something—writing or drawing or something.

One boy lifts up his head and gives me a look. One girl turns around and grins like she's my best friend but she ain't. All a sudden I wish Jamilla was here. Or even J-Boy. He was mean about Buddy and he stole the lawn mower, but he's still somebody I know.

Mrs. Watson squats down beside me and looks me straight in the eye. Her eyes are almost green. "We have six new students because of Katrina," she says. "We've been talking about what happened, and we've decided to make a book. Everybody's doing something to go in it. Would you rather write or draw?"

I don't say anything. I just put my head down on my arms. Then I feel her touching my shoulder. I figure she's already going to send me to the principal. I sit up.

"Why don't you draw?" she says, and hands me a piece of paper and a pack of colored pencils.

She stands up again and walks away.

I look at my paper. Ain't nobody going to help me. It's all on me.

I pick up a black pencil. I draw a dog. Then I draw water.

22

The days pass. In the classroom I sit at the desk. Three of the other Katrina kids move back home before I even find out their names. The ones still left are from someplace else in Mississippi. The only boy is the one who turned around to look at me that first day. His name is Jerome. I find out he hardly ever talks. I find out the grinning girl is named Mattie. I find out there's two kids in my class who don't even speak English. I find out my teacher is going to call me Tyrone no matter what.

It's coming on October. Baby Terrell's giving Mama a fit about trying to climb in the cabinets. One day we lose him and find him stuck up in the cooking pots. She's going around latching everything now. Can't get a glass of water without undoing a lock. One day he gets out the front door and

Mama nearly loses her mind. She looks out and he's rocking down the sidewalk like he knows where he's going. She starts screaming and I go running. When I catch him he's grinning at me like he's proud. I don't fuss at him. I just snatch him up and carry him home and think I'd like to do that, too. Just walk out the front door and not come back.

Tanya's got about a hundred new friends plus a whole stack of new dolls. Everybody's giving them to her. She's got black dolls and white dolls. She's got dolls with hair and dolls without hair. She's got dolls in pink dresses, dolls in bathing suits, and dolls in nothing at all. She's naming them after all her new friends. Every night she kisses every one of them good night. It takes a long time. I lay in my bed and stare at the ceiling while she's kissing.

"Good night, Susie," she says. "Good night, Keisha. Good night, Gaynelle."

Looks like everybody's getting happy except me. And maybe Granpa T. He fixes all the hinges. He takes all the doors down and oils them and sands them and puts them back up. I help him some on a Saturday. Then he crawls up in the kitchen cabinets and puts down new paper all the way to the back corners. He takes apart the stroller somebody gave us and puts it back together again so it rolls twice as good. He looks around and there ain't nothing else to do.

So he sits in the dark and watches the TV.

When I go to school, he's watching the TV. When I come home, he's watching it. When I go to bed, he's still watching it. I ask him what he's watching. He lifts up his hand and says, "This here show," and that's all. Sometime it's about animals in the jungle. Sometime it's about a war somewhere. Mostly it's just people acting stupid.

Mama stands in the kitchen and wipes her hands on a dishrag. "Are you still watching that TV, Granpa T?" she says.

He nods, and she shakes her head. "It's not right," she says. "It's just not right." I sit on my bed and do my homework and learn all my games by heart. I beat every level. I start over.

•◆•

One night at supper seems like everybody's talking at once. Daddy says they're trying out a new way to keep the pine tree resin from gumming up the chain saws. Mama says she's thinking about making some pralines for the bake sale they're having for Tanya's class. Tanya says there's a girl in her class who has hair so long sometimes she sits on it. Baby Terrell reaches over and grabs one of Tanya's ponytails and Tanya screams. When Mama makes him let go, he starts banging his spoon.

I'm thinking I want to bang a spoon. I'm thinking I want everybody to just shut up.

I can't help it.

All a sudden I stand up. I turn around and go in my room and slam the door. Everybody sitting at the table gets real quiet. I hear somebody's chair scrape against the floor. I hear my door open and I flop over fast so I'm facing the wall.

"Son?" It's Daddy's voice.

"Leave me alone!" I yell.

I pull my pillow over my head as quick as I can and wait for the smack.

My room is quiet and I'm waiting. I hear Daddy breathing.

Then I hear the door close real easy, and the voices start up again at the table.

I squeeze my hands into fists and I hit my pillow over and over again until I'm finally too tired to move at all.

•◆•

Don't nobody knock on my door or come in my room for a long time. I lay there in the dark and listen to them clean up the kitchen. When the TV goes on, I hear my door open. The light flips on. I turn over, and there's Granpa T.

"Are you going to lay there like a bump on a log for the rest of your life?"

I don't say nothing.

He sits down on Tanya's bed. "I must be getting old," he says. "I'm always tired."

"I'm tired, too."

"You're young. You ain't got nothing to be tired about. Sit up."

I lift myself up on my elbows.

"That ain't sitting up."

I swing my legs over the side of the bed and sit on the edge. "Is this up enough?"

"Watch your lip."

He's holding his box of pictures. He hands it to me. "Open it."

There's only a handful of pictures inside. They're all of one woman. "You ain't never seen her in person," he says. "Your grandmama passed before your time, but you can see she's the most beautiful woman in the world."

I look at her. She's pretty all right, but she's not the most beautiful woman in the world.

"Her name was Alice," he says.

"I know that," I say.

"She could sing like a bird."

I've heard that, too. Everybody says Tanya's going to sing like that someday.

“Did I ever tell you how I met her?” he says.

I’m thinking, *Probably*, but I don’t say nothing.

“It was Sunday morning, the thirtieth of July, nineteen hundred and sixty-one.”

Here comes a story, I’m thinking, and I sit back.

“I was finally out of the army and back home in Mississippi,” he says. “My pockets were full of money. I bought me a nineteen fifty-nine Cadillac. I was driving right smack through the middle of town. This very town we’re in now.”

He shakes his head. “You should have seen it then. There weren’t more than five or six stoplights and some railroad tracks. Now you can’t get across town in less than half an hour.”

He stops and I wait.

“So I’ve got the windows rolled down,” he starts up again, “and I’m passing by the church. I hear them singing, and I decide to go inside. Turns out every seat is full. I’m standing in the back, holding my hat and wondering how to sneak out, when this girl—” He looks me up and down. “This girl not too much older than you are now, she stands up and starts to sing.”

Granpa T closes his eyes and raises his hands beside his face. “My heart lifts up,” he says. “My heart lifts up on the wings of song.”

He's swaying back and forth real slow like he's listening to something. Then his eyes pop open and he looks at me again.

"When I leave out of that church, Li'l T," he says, "I'm so in love, I swear I'm going to marry that girl if I have to wait a hundred years."

He looks down at the picture for a minute. He's smiling.

"Of course, I had to wait for her to grow up first. I moved on down to New Orleans for a job and before you know it, I was playing the fool. You name it, I did it. I was spending all my money on foolishness. I got the sharpest clothes. I got the sharpest car."

He stops talking and looks at me hard, his eyes squinching up just a little. "I ain't going to tell you about the other stuff. You ain't old enough, and your mama would kill me."

He shakes his head. "Um-hm," he says.

Then he keeps on going. "But even with all that craziness, every Sunday morning, I drove that old car up to Mississippi, and I listened to her sing in the church, and I tried to get her to notice me."

He draws a deep breath. "It didn't work. Even when she got old enough, she wouldn't give me the time of day. I'd speak to her at church. I'd pass by her house in the afternoon. I even wrote her some letters. One day, she finally gave me the lowdown. She said she'd heard all about me. She said she'd heard I didn't have the sense I was born with. She said she had better things planned for her life than passing time with me.

"I remember that like it was yesterday. She was sitting there as sweet and polite as can be. Then she looked up and shot me dead with those words. I jumped in that car, and I went spinning out of her driveway and barreling down the road. It was getting dark and I was somewhere in the woods halfway home when the car just started going slower and slower, and then it stopped.

"Li'l T, I was out of gas. That needle was sitting right on top of that big red E.

"I started cussing. That car wasn't going nowhere soon but I was still jerking at the steering wheel and banging on it and yelling at the top of my lungs."

Granpa T stops talking. He's just sitting there, his mouth closed and his head nodding slightly. Then he looks at me looking at him. "All a sudden, I stopped," he says. "I wiped my face, and I sat there holding on to the steering wheel and looking out at that darkness all around me. And I thought to myself, *Tyrone Elijah Roberts, is this how you want to live your life?* And right then, everything changed.

"I can't explain it. I just know what happened. *I'm a man,*

I thought, *and men don't act like I've been acting. Men take things on their shoulders and carry them.*

"And so I picked up my load. Right then. Right there. And I started carrying it.

"When I got back to New Orleans, I stopped all my foolishness. I saved my money and two years later I bought a house, the very one that just got flooded.

"Six months after that, I carried your grandmama over the threshold. She was wearing a white wedding dress she made herself and a little round hat stuck on with bobby pins. She passed just before your daddy got married."

"How come y'all only had Daddy?"

"That was God's plan."

He ain't looking at the pictures anymore. He ain't looking at anything. "I miss your grandmama," he said. "I miss her every day. She was the most beautiful woman in the world and she could sing like a bird."

We just sit there for a while, looking at the wall.

"Why did you tell me that story, Granpa T?"

He stands up and puts the pictures back in the box. "It's time for you to pick up your load, son."

"I ain't a man, Granpa T."

"You're close," he says. "You're getting awful close."

23

But being a man ain't easy and I can't do it. I go off to school every day and I do my homework like I'm supposed to. I make sure I don't fuss with Tanya and I'm quiet when Baby Terrell's sleeping. But that's all I can do. No matter what, it seems like I can't get happy. My mind can't help flying back to New Orleans, zooming over that black water and trying to see through the roof of our house. It's been almost two months and there ain't no way that bag of food could last that long.

I can't think about that but it's the only thing on my mind.

Then one day toward the end of October Daddy comes home from work and says he's got some news. We're sitting at the table eating, and he says the mayor made an announcement. The mayor says people can come in and look at their houses now. The water's gone way down, but there ain't no electricity and the water in the pipes is poison. There ain't no gas for heating because the flood filled up the gas pipes. There ain't no stores to buy food. There ain't no schools. There ain't no firemen and the National Guard's doing most of the policing.

"But," Daddy says, "the mayor says if we want, we can come in the city. We can go to the house and look. We can look, he says, but we've got to leave. Everybody's got to be out of the city by six o'clock."

"And so?" Mama says.

"And so," Daddy says, "I'm wondering if anybody in this family wants to go look?"

"There's nothing left," Mama says. "There's no point in driving all that way just to look at dead trees and a house rotting into the ground."

Daddy pushes his food around on his plate. Mama makes an airplane fly a couple of green beans into Baby Terrell's mouth.

"I want to go look," Daddy says. "A man at work said he'd give me a ride on Saturday morning. He said anybody wants to go is welcome."

Another airplane load of beans is hanging right outside Baby Terrell's mouth but it ain't going in. Mama stops it in midair. "That's foolishness, T Junior," she says. "We're making a new start here. You're going to let all that rot and ruin drag you down."

"I grew up in that house," Daddy says. "I want to see it. At least one more time."

Mama puts down the plane-load of beans and snatches off Baby Terrell's bib. "Well, I'm not going back," she says. "I'm not ever going back. I don't have the stomach for it." She hoists Baby Terrell out of his seat, and he goes rocking off to his pile of toys.

"What about you?" Daddy's looking at Granpa T. "Don't you want to see your house now?"

Granpa T shakes his head. "I'm too tired," he says.

"It'll be good for you," Daddy says.

Granpa T shakes his head. "I ain't going."

Daddy leans over toward Granpa T. "Come on, Daddy. You need to get out of this apartment. Get up on your feet."

"I ain't going," Granpa says again. "Comes a time, T Junior, when you got to let go."

Daddy leans back. He and Granpa T are looking hard at each other. "I hear what you're saying," Daddy says. "But this ain't that time."

Then everybody's sitting quiet at the table. After a while, I raise my hand like I'm in school. Daddy looks at me.

"I want to see," I say. "I'll go."

Daddy frowns. He knows what I want to see. Then he nods. "Okay. If you were old enough last time, I guess you still are."

•◆•

This time we start out when it's already light. This time I ain't surprised at the broke trees and the air don't smell like a Christmas tree lot anymore. This time Daddy's carrying a cooler with a big lunch packed inside and I'm carrying a box of trash bags.

In the city there still ain't no working traffic lights but it don't matter because there ain't hardly any cars. When we get to where there used to be a light, the handful of cars all stop and take turns going.

Daddy and the man are shaking their heads the whole way. "Look at that," they're saying. "Look at that."

We pass by a house where one side just fell into the street and all the furniture is still sitting there like in a dollhouse. At one store, there's a front loader parked halfway through the front glass window. It's easy to see there ain't nothing left in the store.

A pack of dogs comes trotting around the corner. I sit up straight and look hard. One of them is black but he's got all four legs.

It's hard to figure out where we are because all the signs are down. Finally we pass the corner where the Tomato Man sits. There ain't nothing there. Just sidewalk and weeds. Weeds as tall as me with white flowers on the top.

All the yards are brown. All the grass and bushes are dead. Brown and gray tree branches are piled up as high as my head on the corner lots where they put them after they pulled them out of the streets.

Somebody's fishing boat is sitting on the neutral ground. I see cars knocked every which way—some up in people's yards, some with wheels sitting on the front stoop, some upside down. One looks like it's driving up a tree. It's just standing there on its back end with its front wheels resting high up on the trunk of a big old oak tree. Every single car used to be covered in water. Their windows are smeared over with white and brown mud like they've been painted with it.

Mud is on all the steps and porches. There's a black line going around every house. Actually, there are a bunch of lines, one above the other. That's where the top of the water was, Daddy says. I'm looking at it way above my head. Way above the top of the truck we're sitting in.

All the houses have spray paint marks on the front. They're all the same: A big *X*.

"What's that mark?" Daddy says.

"The rescuers made it," the man says. "They painted one on every house they checked."

We watch the marks go by. We figure out they wrote the date at the top. We figure out they wrote what they found at the bottom. Most houses have a zero at the bottom. We figure that means they didn't find anything. One house says, "Three cats." Another house says, "One dead in attic."

I'm thinking, *One what*? Then I remember Mrs. Washington. I stop looking at the *X*s.

The man pulls up at the corner of our street and drops us off. Now Daddy and me are walking exactly where I walked with Buddy.

It was shady then but now there's too much sun. Half the branches are gone and what are left have been stripped of their leaves.

It was noisy then but now it's quiet. There ain't no sound anywhere except our feet crunching on the little twigs all over the sidewalk. There ain't any cars. There ain't any air conditioners. There ain't any ambulances in the distance or trucks backing up. There ain't any squirrels. There ain't even any birds.

We pass by a pile of trash washed up against somebody's fence. Daddy and me both gag at the same time. The smell is like a wall you walk into. It's like rotten cheese and spoiled chicken and horse droppings and dead rats and other things you don't even want to think about, all sitting there together for weeks and weeks in the hot sun.

We cover our faces and run past but it feels like the smell sticks to us.

We're looking up at all our neighbors' houses. They're all the same. That water mark sits just under the roof line of the one-story houses. Some of the houses have holes chopped in the roof. That's where people climbed out of the attic, Daddy says. Sometimes maybe that's where the searchers climbed in.

On the two-story houses, the water mark is about as high as the floor on the second story.

Our house is a two-story, I'm thinking, and I feel my heart start to pound.

That bathroom is on the second floor, I'm thinking, and I feel my heart go even faster.

And then there it is.

All Mama's flowers and bushes are brown and dead. The driveway is covered up with mud. Half the pecan tree crashed through the attic roof. The other half has smashed the shed. My new bicycle is somewhere under there but there ain't no point in trying to fish it out. It's been crushed and soaked in water for weeks. It ain't going nowhere even if I found it.

The front porch is covered in mud and twisted a little sideways off the front wall.

The swing has come off one chain and is dangling halfway over the rail. The other porch chairs are gone. The pots of plants Mama had on the front steps are busted.

And there is that *X*. There is that *X* painted up above the front porch roof where the rescuers had tied up their boat.

I stand on the street and stare at the *X*.

On the top it says, "9/12."

On the bottom it says, "One dog."

24

We try to push open the front door. It won't budge. Daddy kicks it as hard as he can. It still won't budge.

"It's swoll up," he says.

He steps over to the window opening onto the porch. He's got to be careful of the gap between the porch and house. He takes off his T-shirt and wraps it around his hand. He taps on the glass and breaks it just enough to undo the lock. But when he tries to lift the window, it won't budge either. Finally, he just breaks out all the glass. He's careful to get all the pointy pieces out. He drops them in the hole between the house and the porch. Then he crawls in.

"Sweet Jesus," he says, and I come in after him.

This is the living room. Mama's sofa is upside down on top of the turned-over table. The curtains are pulled off the wall. One set is laying in a heap in the corner. Another set is draped over the TV, which is laying on its back beside the stand it used to be on. The stand is broke to pieces and flat out on the floor. The floor is covered in mud. The rug has floated up and made wrinkles of itself. Underneath the rug, the wood flooring strips are buckled and popping up, and some of them have floated off and got caught in a tangle with the sofa.

Clothes from Granpa T's bedroom are stuck on the floor. A hat is laying upside down by the window. A doll is sitting inside like she's riding in a boat.

The house stinks, and black stuff is growing everywhere. On the cushions and furniture, on the walls and on the ceiling.

When Daddy looks up, he almost laughs. The blades of the ceiling fan are hanging straight down like they melted. They got soaking wet and now they're just drooping down like a dying flower.

I don't even smile when I see it. I'm too busy trying to step over all the stuff. I'm too busy trying to make my way to the stairs.

The stairs ain't safe. When they got wet, they buckled and broke. The rail fell off. We're extra careful climbing up. We press up against the wall where the wallpaper is peeling off in strips. We're in the hall. We can see there was water on the floor. The carpet looks like black bread.

And there's the bathroom. The door is standing wide open. There are scratches all over it. The water in the tub is halfway down and black with scum. Food is scattered everywhere. It smells even worse than the rest of the house with Buddy's business piled up in one corner.

But it don't take even one second to see that Buddy himself ain't in that bathroom no more. Buddy himself is gone.

We're standing there just staring when Daddy sees a piece of paper by the sink. He picks it up.

"It's a note," he says.

I look too. It's so old, the ink is faded away. All we can see of the phone number is 1-800 and then in the middle, a 3. I ball up the paper in my hand.

"He gone," I say.

"But he's still alive somewhere," Daddy says. "Probably. We just don't know where." He puts his hand on my shoulder. "That's got to be enough."

It ain't enough. It ain't even close, but I don't say nothing. I just pull out a trash bag and get to work.

We had planned to fill up the trash bags with trash. But there's so much of that, there ain't any point. So we look for stuff we can keep. We fill up the bags with clothes. We get our own pillows. We get some toys from Baby Terrell's crib. Daddy gets some dolls for Tanya even though I say she has plenty already. I grab up her ballerina skirt and those red shoes. They're still laying on the bed from that day when we were packing.

Daddy's shifting around in his closet when he says, "Oh my God," and I go running in there to see what's wrong.

He's standing there holding a white box. "You know what this is?" he says.

I shake my head.

"It's my mama's wedding dress."

I look at Daddy. His eyes are all full up with water. "Don't cry, Daddy," I say, and then he sits down in the middle of the floor and starts heaving like a little girl. I go over and stand next to him. I put my hand on the top of his head. I'm standing there looking out the window and thinking how round his head is and wondering what am I going to do if he can't stop. What am I going to do if he can't never stop.

And then he stops. He rubs the water out of his eyes and shakes his head and says sorry. He stands up real fast and starts putting clothes in a bag like it ain't never happened. And I figure that's best. It don't change nothing so it ain't never happened.

We throw five bags of clothes and toys in the back of the man's truck when he comes by to pick us up. It's almost six o'clock. We have to hurry. We're barreling out of town and I remember I left that note in the bathroom. It's just as well. I can't read it anyway.

We pull up to the apartment in the dark. The man helps Daddy lift the bags out of the truck. We're saying good-bye and thank you, and Mama and Tanya come running out the front door. They're hugging us and kissing us like we're just back from the war or something. Mama's got fried chicken and lots of tea. I realize I'm about to starve.

We carry the bags in and we're all talking. I'm telling about Buddy and the fan, and Daddy's saying about the wedding dress but not the part where he cried. Tanya is pulling her clothes out of the bag and hugging all those dolls. Granpa T comes wandering in like he's been taking a nap even though it's night. He sits on the sofa and listens to all the jabber. After a while he tilts back his head and goes to his place.

Daddy's telling about how the water filled up the whole downstairs. He's telling Mama about how the kitchen cabinets fell off the walls and the sofa is sitting on top of the table and the refrigerator floated into Granpa T's bedroom.

"Sorry, Daddy," he says to Granpa T. "We couldn't save anything out of your room. Everything downstairs is ruined."

Granpa T don't even move when Daddy says that. He just stays in that place he likes to go.

Daddy looks at Mama. Mama looks at Daddy. Daddy steps over to Granpa T. He touches his shoulder. "Daddy?" he says. "Daddy?"

Granpa T don't move.

I'm watching him while Tanya shakes a toy at Baby Terrell. I'm watching him and then I know Granpa T ain't never going to move again. He's gone to his secret place, and he ain't never coming back.

25

I turn thirteen the day we bury Granpa T. People keep saying it was his time and Katrina broke him and thank the Lord we're in Mississippi with all his people. We put him in the ground in a cemetery that's got broke pine trees standing all around it. Daddy says he's sorry Granpa T has to look at those broke trees forever. He says it's going to remind him for all eternity about Katrina. Mama says don't be a fool. She says Granpa T's sitting at the right hand of Jesus now. He's not thinking about any broke pine trees down here where we are.

Mama says we can't have a cake because of the funeral and I say I don't want one anyway. I say thirteen is too old for all that mess. Mama says no it's not and puts her hand on my shoulder for one teeny second before she tells me to go mind Baby Terrell while she gets Tanya out of her Sunday clothes.

November goes creeping along. Mama says why am I not playing my Game Boy any more and I say I'm too old for that foolishness.

"Well, then," she says, "I guess you're old enough to watch Baby Terrell while I make groceries."

She walks out the door with Tanya tagging behind her and I'm sitting there looking at Baby Terrell squatting on the floor and banging a little plastic hammer on some plastic nails stuck in a plastic workbench.

"You think that's fun?" I say.

He looks up at me and grins. He's got slobber running down his chin and I can tell he already needs his diaper changed.

"What're you so happy about?" I say, and he laughs out loud.

I lay down on the sofa.

"You ain't nothing but a baby," I say. "You ain't got a lick of sense."

At Thanksgiving, Mrs. Watson says we're blessed to be here and says we need to bring in stuff to make give-away bags for the homeless. Mama searches around the apartment and gets some shirts they gave us at the shelter. Then she reaches up under the sofa and pulls out a suitcase. When she opens it up, I see it's Granpa T's clothes, all folded up neat and tidy.

"I ain't taking those," I say.

"But somebody out there needs them," she says.

"Well, I ain't taking them," I say. "You can't make me."

She sits back on her heels and looks at me. "What's wrong with you, son?" she says.

"Ain't nothing wrong with me. I just ain't taking those clothes, is all."

She pushes the suitcase back under the sofa and buys a few extra cans of food at the store.

In our classroom, we pile all the stuff in one corner and we sing a song about something called "sheaves." Jerome asks Mrs. Watson what that is and she says it's a bunch of wheat all held together with a string and I'm thinking why are we singing about that, but I don't say anything.

When we're done singing, Mrs. Watson says to draw a picture of what we are most thankful for.

Daddy says we've got a lot to be thankful for. We're healthy. We've got a roof over our heads. He even managed to buy an old car with some insurance money.

At first, I think maybe I ought to draw a picture of that car. Or maybe of that apartment. Or maybe I ought to draw one of those pictures with everybody all lined up holding hands and write on it, "My Family."

Mrs. Watson would like that.

But a picture like that wouldn't be for true. I'd have to

draw two holes in that picture, and I don't know how to draw an empty space. Besides, I ain't thankful for that empty space.

I look around and everybody's busy drawing. The boy sitting next to me is trying to draw a computer but it don't look too good. That girl Mattie is filling up her paper with flowers but I think that's just because that's what she likes to draw. Jerome is drawing a car, and I know he don't have one. I've seen him after school riding around with the high school brothers, and he ain't the one driving.

I sit there a long time. I can't think of nothing to draw.

Then my pencil starts to move and, sure enough, out comes a dog.

Mrs. Watson's walking around the desks. She stops and looks. "You got your dog back, Tyrone?" she says.

"No, ma'am," I say, "but I'm thankful he's still alive."

•◆•

We're starting the run-up to Christmas. They got candy canes going up on the streetlights in town. When we're in the bus on the way to school, we pass by a mall with a great big old, fake Christmas tree wired onto the top. On the way home, I see the parking lot in that mall is jam-packed with cars and the lights on that tree are blinking on and off.

Mama and Daddy are starting their usual talk about

who knows whether Santa Claus has got anything for us this year. They're mumbling about being good and times are hard and all the same stuff they always say. I say I want some new games for my Game Boy. Mama says why do I want that if I'm too old to play it, and I shrug up my shoulders. Tanya says she want some clothes for her dolls. Baby Terrell just jumps up and down when they sing "Jingle Bells" on the radio.

We get a tree from a lot and I think about the storm and how we hid up under that bed and how when we went outside the whole world smelled like a Christmas tree lot. We stand the tree up in the front window and all a sudden the whole apartment smells like the storm.

Then off we go to the Walmart to get decorations. We're standing there in that aisle and I'm thinking about the stuff we used to stick on the tree. One thing was a white ball I rolled in glitter back in Sunday school. Another was a big old blue star made out of shiny paper with Tanya's picture slap in the middle. And there was a thing I made out of Mardi Gras beads. Something where I glued them all together in a lump and then glued some more to hang down.

We ain't got any of that. We're starting over. Mama buys a pack of red shiny balls and a string of tiny white lights. She says it takes a while to get up a good supply of Christmas decorations. She says we'll get more next year. Then she buys

us some stockings off an aisle that says DISCOUNTED 75%. They look like it, too.

We don't put anything on the bottom part of the tree because Baby Terrell's liable to yank it off. He's walking around now like he owns the place. He don't know there ain't enough stuff on the tree. He don't know there ain't enough presents stacked up underneath. He don't know those flimsy old stockings ought to be hanging off a fireplace instead of off the backs of the kitchen chairs.

We go to a great big church on Christmas Eve. They've got about a hundred people in the choir. They're wearing red robes and singing about Baby Jesus. We're rocking and clapping. Then one lady steps out front and the lights go off and she starts to sing "Silent Night" all by herself. Even Baby Terrell is still.

When we walk out, everybody's smiling and hugging and kissing, and I'm wondering why I ain't happy in the middle of all that love.

Before we go to bed, Daddy gathers us around and we pray. I'm watching him. He's got lines coming down the sides of his mouth. He's got lines between his eyes. He don't know I've seen him in the evening, sitting with his head in his hands, slipping into the kitchen for another beer. I'm watching him, and I bow my head and I pray, too.

In the morning, I sneak into the living room before it's light outside. I always do that. Usually I put a flashlight by my bed the night before but there ain't no flashlight in this apartment so I just go real careful.

I peep around the corner. The living room's empty, of course, without Granpa T sleeping on the sofa. But there those stockings are, hanging off the back of the chairs. They look full of candy. Under Baby Terrell's stocking is some kind of big old baby toy. It looks like a little car you sit in and push around with your feet. Under Tanya's stocking is another doll and a suitcase. I lift up the top real careful. That suitcase is chock-full of doll clothes. And sitting on top is a crown of diamonds just the right size for Tanya. Tanya is going to be one happy girl.

I ain't going to be happy. Under my stocking, there ain't a single thing. Ain't nothing there but floor.

I sit there and look at the empty spot. I'm cold. I'm thinking maybe thirteen is when Santa Claus stops coming. Or maybe I did something bad. I passed all my classes. I take out the garbage. I babysit Baby Terrell. I ain't fussed with Tanya hardly at all the whole time we've been in this apartment. Maybe it's bad to not be happy.

I put my head in my hands, and I'm thinking I look just like Daddy, sitting by myself in the dark with my head in my hands. That living room seems like it gets bigger and emptier the longer I sit there.

And then the light flips on. I turn around and there's Daddy, standing in the door. He ain't got on nothing but his undershorts and his T-shirt. He's rubbing his beard and yawning.

"I thought I heard you," he says.

I don't say nothing.

"You're supposed to wait until morning. We all come in together. Did you forget that?"

"I ain't never waited."

Daddy stops rubbing his face and looks at me. "Never?"

I shake my head.

"You like to get the jump?" he says.

I nod.

He looks at the empty place on the floor. "Didn't turn out so good this time, huh?"

I turn away. I look at the floor.

"Come on," he says soft. "Santa couldn't leave yours out here with the rest. Yours is in our room."

I turn around and look at him.

He's smiling. "Come on," he says again. He flips off the light and heads down the hall.

I get up off the floor and I follow him in the dark.

We go in his room. I smell Baby Terrell's powder. Mama lifts up off her pillow.

"He's wandering around in the dark," Daddy whispers. "He thinks Santa forgot all about him."

Daddy squats down beside his bed. He drags something out from underneath. I can't see it in the dark.

"Hold out your arms," Daddy says, and I do.

And then he puts it in my arms. It's warm. It's wiggly. It's all furry. It lifts up its nose and it licks my face. It starts making little noises and Daddy says, "Take it on out of here before it wakes up Baby Terrell."

"Merry Christmas, son," Mama says, and I can hear in her voice she's smiling.

26

I name that dog Rover.

Mama says, "Why did you name him that?"

I shrug. "It sounds like a dog name."

"Why didn't you name him Li'l B," Daddy says, "for Little Buddy?"

"He ain't Little Buddy," I say. "He ain't even close."

And he ain't. In the first place, he's white with brown spots and Buddy was black. In the second place, he's got short, stiff hair and Buddy's hair was longer and soft when I brushed it. In the third place, he's a yippy, little puppy and Buddy was full grown. In the fourth place, he's got four legs. In the fifth place—

Well, that dog just ain't Little Buddy.

So I call him Rover.

He's got to live in the little bitty apartment with us because we ain't got no yard. He's got a wire cage he sleeps in at night but during the day, he's hopping all over everything. I'm pulling him off Granpa T's sofa and out from under the Christmas tree and out of the laundry basket. And the whole time his tail is going *whap, whap, whap*, and he's looking up at me and grinning like he's proud of all his foolishness.

I sit down with him on the floor to tell him things but he won't stay still. He jumps up on my lap and puts his feet on my chest and tries to lick my face. I push him back on the floor and I say, "Sit still when I'm talking to you." But he don't mind me. He just jumps up again, his tail wagging like he thinks we're playing.

Baby Terrell thinks it's so funny. He rocks over to the dog and goes bop on his back end and when the dog jumps up, Baby Terrell's mouth pops open and he laughs and laughs.

Tanya has to keep pushing him off her dolls. He gets hold of one that's cloth in the middle and pulls off the plastic bottom half of one leg. Tanya's crying like that doll's a real person. I say she has so many she ought to give one to Rover to play with. She's so mad she takes the broke doll and throws it across the room. Rover thinks it's a game. He runs after that doll and grabs it and won't never give it back. It's his now no matter what Tanya says. He sits there with it in his mouth and shakes it at us like he's saying, "Come on and try to take it. Come on and see what happens."

Mama's mouth gets all pinched up and she says, "Li'l T, you're going to have to teach that dog some manners."

I put him on a leash and I take him outside. But I don't know how to teach him manners. He won't listen to me.

Tell the truth, nobody listens to me.

•◆•

It comes on January and I think to myself I ain't never seen a place look so gray. Of course, all the pine trees in Mississippi are broke. What other trees there are got knocked over or their branches got ripped off and besides they ain't got no leaves in the wintertime anyway.

Then it's raining. It ain't like rain in New Orleans. In New Orleans when it rains, it pours—just like it says on the salt box. It fills up the street sometimes, it rains so much. But it don't hardly ever rain all day long. Mostly it rains in the afternoon. It pours for a while, then it clears up, and before you know it, the sun comes out again. In Mississippi, it rains all day long just a little bit. I'm sitting there in that teeny tiny apartment, can't go outside but long enough to let Rover do his business, and I'm thinking how come it can't just come down all at once and get it over with.

Then it's cold. It gets cold in New Orleans, too, but it's only cold for, say, one day. Then it warms up again. Here it's cold for days and days. When school starts up again, Mama says we've got to have coats and gloves. She gets Tanya a coat with what looks like a fur collar. She gets her some gloves with three little balls like a flower stuck on the back of the hand part. Tanya wears that coat and those gloves every day like she's a princess. Mama says what kind of coat do I want and I say I don't want a coat. What am I doing living in a place where I need a coat? Mama says I'm acting like a fool. She says I better straighten up. I say make me, and she purses up her mouth like she's sucking a lemon.

I lay on the sofa and look at the rain and close my eyes. I try my flying trick again but there ain't nowhere to go. Everything I go looking for is gone. Our house. My bicycle. My friends. My dog. I can't pretend I'm sitting at the table drawing pictures with Jamilla or sitting in the shed feeding dog biscuits to Buddy. I can't pretend Buddy's slobbering over his biscuits and his whole body's jerking he's so excited and Granpa T is saying, "Why do you love that ugly, old dog so much?" and Mama's calling me into the house to bag pralines and it's warm outside and the sky is blue and down the street kids are playing and there's music.

I can't pretend because it ain't there no more. Ain't none

of it there no more. When I try my flying trick, I can't even get off the ground.

•◆•

Then it gets to be Valentine's Day. Tanya and Mama make pralines for everybody in Tanya's class. They spend all day Saturday. They ain't got the little bags anymore but Mama wraps each one in cellophane and ties it with a red ribbon. Tanya's cutting hearts out of paper and writing names on them with a red marker. She can't make her *S*'s worth anything. They're mostly backward and that's bad because it looks like almost everybody in her class has an *S* in their name—Sally, Samantha, Sarah, Susan. Mama says do I want some for my class and I just say, "Hmph."

"Well, then take that dog outside," Mama says, "before he drives me crazy."

I tell Rover to drop his doll and he must think I'm telling him to hide it. I finally catch him up under the bed and get a leash on him and out we go.

There ain't nowhere to walk except up and down that six-lane highway but Rover thinks that's the best place in the world. He's snuffling along with his nose glued to the ground and then all a sudden he's heading off toward somebody's patch of grass to dig a little hole. I yank him off that and then he starts trotting down the sidewalk pulling me one way and then the other, barking at birds and barking at cars. I'm thinking it's a good thing he ain't no bigger than a puppy because if he was any bigger, he'd drag me right into the street. When I've had all I can take, we head on back to the apartment and there's Mama with a whole extra box of pralines and a big old grin on her face saying, "We made you some anyway," and I'm supposed to be happy about it.

The next day at school, Mrs. Watson gives everybody in the class a teensy little box of Valentine candy. Some of the girls give her a box back but I leave those pralines in my book bag. Mrs. Watson does a speech on who St. Valentine is and why we've got this day and how it's all about love. Then she leaves off teaching for a little while so we can eat the candy. The boys are all rolling their eyes. They're saying to each other that's the stupidest thing they've ever heard. One brother says, "If I'm going to give a girl something it ain't going to be candy," and everybody laughs. Even me.

After our party Mrs. Watson says we're going to learn to write letters. She goes on and on about what to write where. Then she says we're going to practice. She says to think of somebody we ain't talked to in a long time. We can write a letter to that person and Mrs. Watson will put in the mail for us.

I know exactly who I'm going to write. I pick up my pencil

and I get going. "Dear Jamilla," I write, "Why haven't you answered my letters?" Then I tell her all about everything. It takes me three pages of writing front and back. I don't even stop to look up. At the end I do just like Mrs. Watson says and I write, "Sincerely, Li'l T." That looks stupid, though, so I erase it and change it to "Love, Li'l T." But that ain't right neither. So I erase it one more time and just write "Li'l T." That seems like it ought to be enough. I write all the address I can remember on the envelope and hand it in to Mrs. Watson. Then I give Mrs. Watson the whole box of pralines to take home for herself.

•◆•

Two weeks after that Mrs. Watson calls me up to her desk at lunch. She's holding that letter in her hand. She gives it back to me.

It has two words stamped on the front. "Insufficient Address."

"Chicago is a big city," she's saying. "You need more than just the street. You need the house number, too."

"I don't know it," I say.

"Do you have it written down at home?"

"All that stuff's gone."

"Gone?"

I shrug. “Washed away.”

“Don’t you know her phone number?”

I shake my head.

“Does she know yours?”

“She don’t know where we’re living now.”

Mrs. Watson and I just stare at the letter. It looks all dirty now, not clean and white like when I sent it off.

“I guess—” I stop talking and shrug. “I guess there ain’t no way to send it then.”

She shakes her head. “But keep it,” she says.

“I don’t want it,” I say, and start tearing it in half.

“Don’t do that, Tyrone. It’s a beautiful letter.”

“She’s gone,” I say. “Granpa T says comes a time—”

I rip that letter into so many pieces it looks like a pile of confetti laying in the bottom of the trash can. Mrs. Watson’s watching me the whole time. Then I walk outside and stand in the cold and rain all by myself. Right before the bell rings, that boy Jerome comes up to me and looks me over.

“What’re you doing standing here all by yourself?” he says.

“Thinking.”

“About what?”

“Stuff.”

He hikes up his pants a little and looks me over again.

"Some of us are getting together after school. There's a place behind the Winn-Dixie. We've got some weed. You want to come?"

I don't turn my head to look at him. I keep my eyes on the jungle gym. There's a girl hanging upside down and laughing.

"I can't," I say.

"How come?"

"Got work."

He nods. "Next time maybe."

I nod back and he walks away.

27

The next time Mrs. Watson calls me up to her desk it ain't about a letter. This time, she asks real quiet why I ain't done my homework. I shrug my shoulders and look out the window. She says I was doing so good at the first of the year and now I ain't. She says is anything troubling me, and I say, "No, ma'am." She says, "Well, go finish this homework now. You'll need this study sheet for the test. I'll look over it after lunch."

I sit back down at my desk. "What is the capital of Peru?" the question says. "Who was the first explorer to cross the Andes?" "List the three main exports of Brazil." I put my head down on my desk. I fall asleep. When I wake up, there's a wet spot on the paper and I've missed my lunch.

•◆•

The day before Mardi Gras, Mama leaves out to buy a King Cake the minute I come home from school.

"You watch Tanya and Terrell," she says, "and I'll go find us a King Cake. We might as well get whatever Mardi Gras we can get."

Tanya says she wants chocolate cream, and I say I want plain, and Mama says we don't get to choose. She says she'll just get what she can get, and we better be happy.

But ain't nobody in that town sells King Cake. She's gone a long time, and when she comes back empty-handed, we can't believe it.

We're sitting at the table that night and Daddy's saying what made Mama think they've got King Cake in a place like this, and Mama says she hasn't ever been anywhere in her life where they don't have King Cake.

And Daddy says, "That's because you ain't never been out of New Orleans."

And Mama says, "Well, where all have you been, Mr. World Traveler?"

And Daddy says, "You forgot I was in the service. I've been all kinds of places."

And Mama says, "So I guess you're smarter than everybody else sitting at this table?"

And Daddy starts to say something back, and then he stops.

Everybody at the table gets real quiet.

I look at Daddy and I see he's looking at Mama.

"It's going to be all right," he says to her. "We're going to make it."

Mama nods her head a little bit and pinches up her lips, and then she says, "It's not about the cake." She turns her head and looks at me. "It's about Li'l T."

All the eyes swivel around to look at me.

"What about Li'l T?" Daddy says, and I know he's thinking he ain't got a stick in this apartment.

"I was going to wait until after we ate," Mama says, "but I might as well go ahead now." She looks toward the window for a second then starts up again. "I didn't go out just to buy King Cake. I went by Li'l T's school, too."

She looks back at me. "They called me this afternoon," she says. She ain't taking her eyes off me. Ain't none of them taking their eyes off me. "They say he hasn't been at school today. They say he's getting *F*s."

I feel like I'm sitting in a fire. I feel like the end of the world has come.

"Is that true, son?" Daddy says.

I look down at my hands resting on top of my napkin.

My fingers are all twisted in a knot. I can't hardly move but I'm just barely able to nod my head.

"Look at me," Daddy says.

I manage to raise up my head and look at his shirt.

"Look me in the eye."

I lift up my eyes and there's his face. There are his eyes looking straight at me.

"Where did you go?" he says.

"The mall," I say.

"What did you do at the mall?"

"Walk. Sit."

"Who were you with?"

"Nobody."

He's looking at me hard. His eyes are all squinched up. Tanya's eyes are big as saucers. Baby Terrell picks up his spoon and throws it on the floor. Mama bends down and picks it up and wipes it off.

"Is that the truth?" Daddy says.

"Yes, sir."

"Go to your room. The rest of us are going to finish eating."

I stand up. My chair makes a noise. I start to push it back to the table and then I give up. I go in my room and I shut my door. I lay down on my bed, and I can't believe it. I start to cry. I cry and cry and cry and cry. I stop for a while and then I start up again. I cry with my pillow on my head and without it. I curl up in a ball and then I flop around like one of Tanya's cloth dolls. I cry quiet and I cry loud.

And all that time, nobody comes in the room. Not even Tanya. When I'm finally done, it's way past bedtime and I need to go to the bathroom. The whole apartment is quiet. I open my door and it don't squeak a bit. I do my business and when I'm back in the living room again, I nearly jump out of my skin. There's Granpa T, stretched out on the sofa and looking straight at me. My heart stops.

He sits up, and then my heart starts beating again because I see it ain't Granpa T at all. It's Daddy.

"Son," he says. "Sit down."

That dog Rover ain't in his wire cage. He's all curled up at Daddy's feet. When I sit down, he lifts up his head and his tail goes *whap, whap*.

"What do you want in life, son?" Daddy says.

I don't answer.

"Whatever it is, skipping school ain't the way to get it."

I still don't say nothing.

"Tomorrow I'm taking you to school. I'm going to walk with you to see the principal. I'm going to walk with you to see your teacher. But I ain't always going to be around to take those hard walks with you. This is just practice for when you have to do it by yourself."

He waits for me to say something but I ain't got nothing to say.

"I'm going to miss some work and it's going to cost us some money. So you've got to pay us back."

I raise up my head and look at him.

"I'm going to New Orleans this weekend. I've decided I'm going to start mucking out the house. Mama don't like it, but I've decided I'm going to do it. And you're going to help me. All day Saturday. On Sunday, you're going to sit in this apartment and you're going to study. You can't make up those tests but you can learn what was on them.

"Every time I go to New Orleans from now on, you're coming and you're working. You're working hard and you're working for free. Every Sunday from now on, you're studying and you're studying hard.

"Ain't no *F* going to come through the door of my house. Ain't no 'skipping school' going to sit at my table."

I'm shivering in the cool, but I don't move.

"You understand what I'm saying?"

"Yes, sir."

"You got anything you need to tell me, son?"

I'm quiet for a little while. Then I find my voice. "Some of the brothers are smoking weed behind the Winn-Dixie after school. They asked me to come. But I ain't done that, Daddy. And I won't. I promise."

I can tell Daddy's looking hard at me in the dark. "Can I trust you, son?"

"Yes, sir."

He nods. "Anything else?"

"When I saw you laying on the sofa, I thought you were Granpa T." I can't believe it. My voice gets all bumpy when I say that.

Daddy don't say nothing for a while. Then he sucks in a deep breath. "Go on to bed," he says. "It's cold."

I stand up. Rover hops off the sofa, too.

Daddy watches me walk to the door of the bedroom. When I push it open, Rover zips inside and jumps up on my bed. I don't push him off. I lay down beside him. I hear Daddy's voice talking to Mama in the other room. I hear Rover snuffling his nose once or twice.

I put my hand on his back and I go to sleep.

28

That first day we go back to New Orleans, Daddy works me so hard I think he's going to kill me. We're dragging all the wet, black stuff out of the house and piling it up by the street. We can't hardly carry the sofa between us, but somehow we manage. We stand in Granpa T's room for about an hour staring at the refrigerator laying facedown on the floor and trying to figure out how to move it. Daddy's afraid to lift it up because whatever is in it will fall out. But we can't just leave it laying there forever. Finally we give up and go back to work in the living room on the stuff we know how to do—the tables and chairs and dishes and clothes and pictures and curtains and books. By the end of the day, there's a heap of stuff as tall as me stretching all the way across the sidewalk in front of our house.

We're standing on the street looking at that pile. We're filthy from our heads to our feet. Daddy's grinning about as big as I've seen since August. "We started," he says. "I guess we can finish."

I ain't so sure but I don't say nothing. When we get home, I just open my book bag and start studying.

The next Saturday, we clean out Granpa T's room except for the refrigerator. I'm worrying it's going to be sad to do, but it ain't. We can't even tell all that stuff was ever his. I collect up what pictures are still hanging on the wall, except they ain't pictures anymore. They're just frames with glass in them and streaky, colored paper behind. The hanging rod in his closet broke and all his shirts and suits are wadded together in a heap on the floor on top of his old shoes. That old mattress weighs a ton, being full of water. The drawers in the bureau are stuck shut so we just haul the whole thing out at once.

We go back inside and stand in Granpa T's room just looking. It's so quiet in New Orleans now that when we ain't making noise ourselves my ears feel like they fill up with silence, like there ain't no such thing as sound.

Then Daddy sucks in a deep breath. "Well," he says, "at least we still got some pictures of your grandmama."

I don't say nothing because there really ain't nothing to say.

•◆•

The next weekend we have a bunch of helpers. We wrap the refrigerator around and around with duct tape and set it on the street. One of the helpers thinks he's so funny. He gets a marker out of his truck and writes all over the refrigerator, FREE KATRINA GUMBO INSIDE! SPECIAL RECIPE! Everybody stands around and laughs for a little bit. Then we go inside and drag out the washer and dryer, still sloshing with water inside them.

I'm carrying a load of rotten towels to the street when along comes this big old truck. It's got a claw arm attached behind the cab. It pulls up in front of our house and that claw arm reaches out and latches on to the refrigerator. It lifts it up like it's a toy, turns it a little this way and a little that way, and sets it down in the back of that truck with about fifteen other refrigerators all lined up like they're on sale, except they're not. And then off it goes, looking for another dead refrigerator.

When we get home that night, I'm telling all about the refrigerator truck and this other truck that came along with a little Bobcat. That little Bobcat hustled up to our washer and dryer and picked both of them up at the same time—side by side just like they always were in the house. It carried them to the truck and set them down in the trailer and off they went, side by side forever.

Tanya falls out laughing, and then Baby Terrell grabs one of her dolls and whops her, and Mama starts fussing, and Daddy shakes his head, and Rover starts barking, and to tell truth, I can't help but laugh a little bit myself. I laugh and then I get out my books.

•◆•

A couple weeks after that, Daddy say's there's so much work to do, we're going to start staying overnight soon as my grades get better.

"They're already better," I say. "School ain't hard."

"Then you're a bigger fool than I thought making *F*s."

"I ain't making *F*s no more. I'm up to *B*s now."

"Then I guess we can stay overnight. You can bring your books with you. But if you go down—"

"I ain't going down. I promise."

Mama's standing there listening with her arms crossed over her chest. "So now you'll be gone Saturday and Sunday," she says.

"I guess," Daddy says.

"Then you can take that dog with you. Nobody's taught him any manners yet, and I can't watch him and my babies, too."

Baby Terrell's kicking to get down out of his high chair.

Mama picks him up and while she's still holding him, she turns around and looks at Daddy.

"Why are you doing all this, T Junior?" she says.

"We're going home, baby," Daddy says. "When I get that house fixed up, we're going home."

•◆•

So Daddy and me start camping in the old house on Saturday nights. We get us a couple of air mattresses and a battery-operated lantern and a cooler so big I can almost lay down in it. Daddy fixes up a kind of hideaway spot in the backyard where we can do our business and we're ready to go.

Mama cooks us something to take that we can eat cold. We stop at a store on the way in and get a supply of drinks and two gallons of water. Daddy always has it figured out what we're going to do. Maybe we'll be tearing out the plaster in the living room. Maybe we'll be ripping out the carpet. When it gets too dark to work, we each get one gallon of water to wash up. Then we eat what Mama cooked, stretch out on those air mattresses, and don't move until morning.

Not even Rover. He spends the whole day hunting rats in the yard or keeping cool under the house. When we wash up, he stands under the drips and tries to bite them. When we go to sleep, he snugs himself down in a spot he's made under the house right below my mattress. Soon as he hears my feet hit the floor in the morning, his tail starts whopping on the dirt, and then we get busy all over again.

One Saturday Daddy sets me to work in the old bathroom banging out the tiles and adding them to the pile in front. He gives me a little mallet and a face mask and he tells me to knock off every last piece. Daddy goes over to Mrs. Washington's house to help some men from the church get her refrigerator wrapped up and on the street. Her nephew's coming back soon they say and at least that much will be done.

I'm swinging that mallet like there's no tomorrow and sweating hard. Those tiles are flying. Every once in a while I stop and catch my breath and then I get going again. That bathroom's getting full of dust. I'm finding the same thing on every stud—black mold growing at the bottom. Daddy says when we get everything cleared out, we're going to wash every stick of wood in that house with bleach. That's going to be some kind of hard job.

Eventually, there's so much dust in there I can't hardly see. I'm covered in white from head to toe. I decide it's time to take a break. I go outside to sit on the front porch.

Soon as the screen door bangs, Rover comes zipping around from the backyard. He loves coming to New Orleans.

He kills a rat twice a day almost, and that's way more fun than dragging that old doll around. Sure enough, he's carrying something dead now and he wants me to see it.

"Put that down, you fool dog," I say.

He just stands there looking at me, his tail slowing down a little bit.

"You can't come up on the porch with that," I say, and his tail starts going again. He takes one step forward and I hustle down the steps.

"Drop it!"

He don't budge.

"You got to learn, Rover," I say. "We just can't have dead rats lined up on the porch anymore. Drop it."

He's kind of whining and trying to decide what to do. I'm thinking I wish he spoke English. I wish he knew what to do like Buddy did. I wish somebody had trained him.

And then—*pow!*—it hits me. Ain't nobody trained Rover because he ain't never been anybody else's dog before he was mine.

I'm standing there looking at that dog and his tail whapping away and that dead rat hanging out of his mouth, and I'm thinking, *It's all on me.*

He's watching me right back and his tail is speeding up.

I notice his eyes are sort of like Buddy's. They're dark, dark brown and they've got black going all around them. Rover stretches out his front feet and bends down and looks up at me, and I can't decide whether he's laughing at me or not.

"Drop it," I say, making my voice sound like Daddy. I point to the ground.

Rover ducks down a little farther. He shakes his head like I must think he's a fool if I think he's going to let go of that rat.

And then—*boom*—he drops it.

I can't believe it. I go down on my knees. His eyes ain't laughing at me at all. They're just laughing. I rub him all along his neck and say, "Good dog. Good dog, Rover."

Then he's trying to climb me, and it's all I can do to stay out of the way of his tongue and his scratching, wet paws when all a sudden I hear somebody say, "That ain't Buddy."

I whip around and there's J-Boy, standing at the gate.

My heart leaps up in happiness. "You're home!" I say.

"Yeah," he says, and nods his head a little. "I'm home."

I'm standing up, and Rover's jumping on me and still licking me and letting out little barks, and I'm trying to push him down, and he thinks it's all a game just like Baby Terrell when he whops you with his toy and thinks it's so funny.

"That ain't the three-legged dog," J-Boy says. "What happened to him? He drown?"

I don't feel like answering that. I push Rover down again, and lucky for me and J-Boy, he hears something scratching under the house and goes sniffing after it.

We stand there a minute, watching Rover's back end sticking out from under the house and his tail whacking back and forth. When I look up at J-Boy, I see his eyes are half-closed and he's got a piece of lint stuck in his hair.

"Where have you been?" I ask him.

"We ended up in Houston."

"We're in Mississippi. But we're coming home once we fix up the house. Are you fixing your house?"

"Nah," he says. "It ain't our house anyway."

"Where're you staying then?"

He nods his head to the side a little. "Down the street."

"Where're you going to school?"

"I ain't."

"You ain't going to school?"

"I'm finished with school."

"You graduated?"

He rolls his eyes. "You always was a fool. I'm sixteen. I don't have to go anymore. I'm through with school."

"You're sixteen?"

"Almost."

"When will you be sixteen?"

"Ain't none of your business."

"Your mama says you can quit school?"

"Ain't none of her business."

"She ain't calling the cops on you?"

"She ain't here. She's in Houston."

"So you're staying in New Orleans by yourself?"

"I got company."

"Your mama says that's okay?"

"She can say what she wants. I don't care."

We're standing there at the gate just looking at each other. Then he looks up at the house. "So you're living here now?"

"No. I told you. We're just here on the weekend. Then we go back to Mississippi."

"You fixed the roof," he says.

"Daddy mostly did that."

"You got electricity?"

I laugh. "You're the fool now."

He looks up the street. "I got to go." He hikes up his pants and he eases off.

I sit down on the porch. I look at all the houses up and down my street. There ain't nobody living in any of them. I wonder where that boy Rusty is now. And where is that boy I never talked to that was always reading books. And that girl who was taller than me but who was nice. And my teacher. And all the other kids and all the other teachers. Of all those people, I'm thinking, why is J-Boy the only one who's made it back?

29

When it gets to be almost Easter, Mama says, "You aren't going to New Orleans for Easter Sunday, are you?"

"I'm going to church on Easter," Daddy says, "but I'm going to my church in New Orleans. Me and Li'l T, we'll take a break long enough to go to church."

Mama's standing with her hands on her hips.

"Do you want to come with us?" Daddy says.

"And what am I going to do with a toddler baby in a house full of rusty nails and holes?"

Daddy shrugs up his shoulders. "Suit yourself," he says.

"I think you're crazy," Mama says, "living in an empty city in a rotten house with a half-wild dog and a boy no more than thirteen years old."

Daddy looks at me. "Do you think I'm crazy, Li'l T?"

I shake my head.

Mama stomps off to the kitchen.

Daddy sits there watching her walk off. Then he looks at me. "Sometimes, Li'l T," he says, "you just got to do what you got to do, even if it don't make sense to anybody but you."

"It makes sense to me, Daddy."

Daddy shakes his head. "But not to your mama."

•◆•

When we pull up on Easter weekend, Rover jumps out of the car and shoots straight for the back, barking up a storm.

Daddy laughs. "He's already after a rat."

We unlock the front door, Daddy walks in, and all a sudden he starts up saying things I can't write down in this story. I'm right behind him but he holds out his hand to keep me back.

"Don't look, Li'l T," he says, but I look anyway.

There's a man laying on one of our air mattresses. There's food trash laying all around him. There are needles and plastic tubes and spoons. There are candles all burned down. There are rags piled up in one corner. There are six empty wine bottles lined up under the window.

"Is he dead?" I say.

Daddy inches over to him and pokes him with his toe.

The man opens his eyes. He looks up at Daddy.

"Get out of my house," Daddy says.

The man stands up and I see he's not a man, not quite.

"And take all this—stuff—with you."

The boy don't say anything. He's just looking at us. Then he looks down at everything laying around the room. "I don't want it," he says. Then he stumbles out the door.

Daddy's following right behind him. The boy gets to the steps and Daddy hollers after him, "If I ever see you in my house again, I'll kill you. You hear what I'm saying?"

The boy waves his hand at us like we're mosquitoes or something. He grabs hold of the fence so he won't fall and then he heads on down the street.

We're standing there watching him go. "That's the dregs, Li'l T," Daddy says. "Now we have to clean up after him."

Except Daddy won't let me touch anything. He says I'm too young. He tells me to go on to work in the kitchen. We've got to haul out those cabinets this weekend. I go in the kitchen. I see the kitchen door has been broke open and there's another nest with our other mattress and all the same stuff.

I holler to Daddy, "There was two of them."

Daddy comes and looks. "You suppose this one was just a boy, too?" he says. He pokes his toe in the rags. "What are we coming to, Li'l T, if our children are living like this?"

I look up and Rover is standing there in the back door with a shoe in his mouth and grinning like he thinks it's a rat.

"Drop it," I say, and he does.

I rub him all up. I tell him he's a good dog and throw the shoe back out in the yard. "Now go find a real rat," I say, and slap him on the behind.

He hops off down the steps, sniffing and jumping and barking and wagging his tail like there's no tomorrow.

I stand there on the back stoop, looking across the backyards with all their crushed fences and collapsed sheds and upside down cars. It's so quiet on the street, I can hear music playing a long way off. And then I hear a bird, the first one I've heard in New Orleans since the storm. From somewhere in somebody's backyard, he's singing and singing. I don't look for him. I just close my eyes and listen.

Easter morning, we wake up early in our camp in our house. Daddy says we got to go to the sunrise service even if there ain't no sunrise to see inside the building. We don't dress up. Daddy says people in New Orleans don't worry about that stuff now. I'm following him out the front door when I realize the Easter Bunny didn't come. I'm wondering if maybe there's a basket for me at the apartment. And then

I hope not. I hope the Easter Bunny knows I'm too old for that stuff now.

Me and Daddy walk real quiet into the church. It's darkish in there but that church is full of people. Daddy puts his hand on my shoulder and guides me to a seat near the front just like where we used to sit.

I hear the people all around me breathing.

Then the light starts to come in through the windows. It's coming in slow and steady. The sun is rising and we're all sitting there waiting.

All a sudden I hear a big rustle and a bunch of people at the front of the church stand up.

Then I hear a voice lift up in song. It's Brother James. And then the people behind him join in. And the church fills up with light and we all stand up. All of us. And I look around.

It's all different kinds of people. Some faces I know, but there are lots of faces I ain't never seen. Black faces. White faces. Young faces. A few old faces.

"Who are all these people?" I whisper to Daddy.

"They're our neighbors," he says.

"But I thought nobody was here."

"You thought wrong," he says, and we start singing, too.

When that service is over, everybody comes pouring out the door, hugging and kissing and praising God right and left.

There's a man standing off in the shade of the porch wearing army clothes. Daddy goes up to him and shakes his hand and pats him on the shoulder.

"I'm sorry," Daddy says. "She was a fine woman. A good woman."

Then I know that's Mrs. Washington's nephew. He's back from Iraq but she ain't there to see him.

Now he's nodding his head and pressing his fingers in his eyes. "I miss her," he says real quiet.

"It's like that sometimes," Daddy says, and pats his shoulder again.

Then up comes Mr. Nelson. "Whoo-eee!" he says, and stops right in front of me. "This ain't Li'l T!" he says.

"Sure is," Daddy says, and they're shaking hands and hugging and talking about how Houston's a fine place, but it ain't New Orleans, and Daddy's glad to be working but he wants to come home something awful. And Mr. Nelson's house only had three feet of water but it was ruined. And—God be praised—the church is okay. And where's our family anyway? And how is old Mr. Roberts? And then they're quiet and Mr. Nelson says, "May he rest in peace."

Then Mr. Nelson looks at me and says all over again, "I know this ain't Li'l T!"

"It sure is," Daddy says again.

"What are you feeding him, T Junior?" Mr. Nelson says. "He's done shot up like a weed."

"He's got a good start," Daddy says, "but he's got a ways to go."

"You're going to be like your grandpa, boy," Mr. Nelson says, "tall and skinny."

"I'm tall!" Daddy says.

"But you ain't skinny!" Mr. Nelson says, and now everybody's laughing and slapping each other on the arm, and then Mr. Nelson turns to me and says, "How about that three-legged dog? Where is he at?"

And all a sudden I feel like it ain't spring anymore.

Daddy looks at me and puts his hand on my shoulder. Mr. Nelson ain't laughing now.

"We had to leave the dog behind," Daddy says. "He's gone."

"But he ain't dead," I say, looking down at my shoes. "He's alive somewhere. We just don't know where."

"I'm sorry, son," Mr. Nelson says. He shakes his head. "So much is gone. I'm sorry I asked."

30

Before we know it, school is over. Mrs. Watson's giving me a hug and saying she's so proud of me and I've got a lot of potential and all kinds of stuff like teachers always say. I'm just thinking what am I going to do this summer, sitting in that apartment all day every day.

The whole family goes to a party where the kindergarteners graduate to first grade. All Tanya's friends are wearing big bows in their hair and holding hands. The teacher gives Tanya a piece of paper with a giant smiley face on it saying she's an honor student—in kindergarten.

Daddy and Mama want to be happy but they can't because Daddy's job clearing out all those broke trees is over. What they can do, they've done.

When we get home that night, Daddy and Mama sit

together at the table in that little apartment. They got the newspaper spread out in front of them and every once in a while they make a circle around a notice for a job. Daddy's shaking his head. Mama's wrapping her hands together.

"What are we going to do now?" she says.

Daddy folds up the newspaper. He sits back. He crosses his arms over his chest. He looks Mama in the face. "We're going to go home," he says.

And so we do.

•◆•

We can't move into the house to start. It ain't close to ready. No rain can get in because we fixed the roof where the pecan tree came through. A bunch of men from the church helped us get the front porch straightened out, and we got it mostly mucked out. But it ain't got hardly no inside walls, and the outside walls are just the weatherboard nailed on the studs. Mama won't even come look at it much less live in it, especially once she hears about the squatters.

Brother James fixes up a place for her with a widow two streets over. That widow's old and she needs somebody to look after her. Mama can do that while she's chasing Baby Terrell. Mama says maybe the widow will let her use the kitchen to make a few pralines again. And if she's going to be cooking for the widow, maybe she can cook up a few lunches to sell to the people working on the houses.

The problem is that the widow's only got one extra bedroom. Daddy's got to sleep in the old house or on the street. I say I'll sleep with him in the house. Mama says over her dead body. She says it ain't safe. Daddy says it's us being there that's going to make it safe, and besides we like camping out.

He's tee-heeing about that, but Mama ain't laughing at all. After a while, though, she nods her head. "Okay," she says. "I guess you're going to do what you're going to do."

So Mama and Tanya and Baby Terrell move into the old lady's extra room, and Daddy and Rover and me move into the old house full-time. Rover thinks he's in heaven getting to chase rats every day. The good thing is, he don't line them up on the porch anymore, and I've just about taught him not to jump all over me, especially when he's got one hanging in his mouth.

Daddy ain't got no regular job, but he's picking up day work gutting houses and clearing lots. He works on the old house whenever he can scrape up enough money to buy some boards or nails or whatever else he needs. He gives me projects every day when he's gone. I'm getting good at ripping stuff out. Next he's going to teach me how to hang Sheetrock.

Summer is almost halfway over, and truth be told, that house don't look much different.

Daddy's starting to sit with his head in his hands again. He's starting to get those lines in his face.

Then one afternoon I look up from where I'm nailing down a loose board on the front porch and here comes Mama with Tanya and Baby Terrell. They ain't never been by before, not the whole time since we've been back. Tanya's wearing her crown and holding Baby Terrell by the hand. Mama's pulling an old, rusty wagon. Inside that wagon are two great big cooking pots and a cardboard box full of paper bowls, napkins, and plastic forks with a great big old loaf of white bread laid over the top. Stuck on the side of the box with tape is a sign that says, MAMA'S HOME COOKING. I can tell Tanya colored it because the *S* is backward.

"There's two servings still left," Mama says, "and I won't charge you."

She puts down the handle of the wagon and picks up Baby Terrell. Tanya grabs hold of her skirt.

Then Mama just stands in the yard and looks. I see her eyes going up to the big *X* above the front porch roof. She looks at me and she looks at that *X* and I know what she's thinking.

Tanya's lifting up her thumb toward her mouth.

"Don't stick that in your mouth," I say.

Tanya jumps and stares at me. "You ain't my daddy," she says.

I lift up my hand like I'm going to wallop her, and Mama says, "Li'l T, I thought you were older than that."

I let my hand down. I feel ashamed and I feel sad.

Then I look up at the house with them. I ain't noticed before how the yard is all full of weeds and they're almost tall as me. I ain't seen the way the grass is growing up through cracks in the sidewalk and practically covering it up. I ain't noticed the way the paint is peeling off in great big old chunks the size of my hand all the way up the side of the house to where that water mark is still a dirty, black line. It's been a long time since I noticed that the bushes up by the porch are just dried-up brown sticks or that the stump of the pecan tree is all covered over with cat's claw vine and morning glory.

Then along comes Rover galloping like a racehorse around the corner of the house. He skids to a stop in front of us with his tongue flopping out and his tail going a mile a minute. He ain't seen Mama and them since we started camping in the old house. He bounces around on his feet and barks. Mama almost smiles.

"That dog's grown," she says.

Baby Terrell's trying to jump out of her arms. She's

holding on to him the best she can. "You can't get down," she says. "It's too dangerous."

"No!" he shouts, and we all stop in our tracks and look at him.

"Did he say *no*?" I say.

Mama's looking at him like she's proud. "Did you say *no*?" she says. "Did you say that, Baby Terrell?"

He's flopping himself hard. "No!" he yells again. "No! No! No!"

Then we're all laughing and Mama finally puts him on the ground. "I guess if you can talk, I better let you walk. Li'l T, don't let him out of your sight. I'm going to have a look at this old house. I guess I have to."

Mama goes inside, and Daddy's hammer stops. She stays inside a long, long time. I eat a bowl of red beans and rice and three pieces of bread. I throw a stick for Rover. He runs to pick it up and brings it back. Baby Terrell claps his hands. We do it all again. Tanya's sitting on the steps. She's sitting on her hands so her thumb won't accidentally slide into her mouth. Rover goes running up to her and jumps on her and her crown almost falls off.

"Bad dog," she says. "Go away," she says, but she's laughing.

"Say *down*," I tell her. "He don't understand *go away*."

She's too busy straightening up her crown to pay any attention.

"Ba, ba, ba, ba, ba," Baby Terrell says.

Then I look up and there's Mama, standing in the front door. She's standing there looking at us sitting on the steps. She looks at Tanya and she looks at me and she looks at Baby Terrell. We're looking back at her.

"What are you staring at?" she says all a sudden.

"Your face is all wet," Tanya says.

Mama reaches up and rubs her hand across her cheeks.

"Now it's dirty," Tanya says.

Mama closes her eyes and takes a big breath. "And you think that's funny, I guess."

Tanya shakes her head real slow.

"It's okay, Mama," I say. "It's going to be all right."

"You aren't old enough to tell me that," she snaps back at me. "Besides I've got something to tell you. Me and Tanya are going to take that wagon and walk to the store. I've got enough cash in my pocket right here to buy us a couple jugs of bleach and some scrub brushes. You're going to watch Baby Terrell. When we get back, we're going to set up Tanya and Baby Terrell in the front room where he can't get loose. And then you and me are going to start washing the wood. I figure if I don't start helping out, this house isn't ever going to be done. Come on, Tanya. You're going to carry the brushes."

•◆•

Mama don't like working with that bleach. Daddy teases her and says she's going to turn white. She says if she does it'll only be in spots and that'll make her a leopard and he better watch out if he gets too close.

Daddy laughs out loud and Mama smiles a little, and I just keep on scrubbing.

Daddy's got an electrician lined up to come fix the wires as soon as it's all washed. A man from the church is going to help with the pipes. Then we can start hanging the Sheetrock. Things are finally moving along.

One day I'm taking a break from scrubbing and sitting outside watching Baby Terrell with Tanya when I look up and there's Brother James, standing just inside the gate.

"Your mama and daddy inside?" he says.

"Yes, sir."

"Go get them. I've got something to tell y'all. I'll watch the baby."

I go inside. The house is dark and quiet. Little spots of dust are floating in the air where the sun's coming through the cracks. Then I hear their voices. They're upstairs. I climb up the creaky stairs. When I get there, they ain't scrubbing. They're standing in their bedroom except it ain't got any walls. They're hugging.

"Brother James is here," I say. "He says go get you."

"Brother James?" Daddy says.

Mama rubs her hand across her face. "How do I look?" she says.

"Strong," Daddy says.

We walk out on the porch and Brother James is bouncing Baby Terrell up and down on his knee like Granpa T used to do. Baby Terrell's laughing and squealing and Tanya is squinched over to one side, smiling and sitting on her hands.

Everybody says their hellos and finds a shady place to sit.

"Y'all get to watch much TV?" Brother James says.

Daddy laughs a little. "Ain't got no electricity, Brother James. Can't watch much TV that way."

"True." Brother James nods. "Then y'all probably didn't see that show last night."

We're all shaking our heads.

"It was about Katrina."

We all make faces.

"It was about the rescuers. The ones who saved the dogs."

I sit up.

"There must have been a hundred different groups that

came in and saved those animals. They were telling about how they found cats and birds and dogs—especially dogs—all left behind. They said at first they thought the people had just abandoned their pets. They thought the people just didn't love them."

"But our car was too little!" I say. "We thought we'd be right back!"

"They figured it out," Brother James says, and nods. "They're smart people. They figured it out."

We're all sitting there real quiet just looking at the dead yard. Rover is poking his nose in the stick bushes and piles of trash. His tail is going back and forth like it's attached to an engine. He bends down on his front legs and whines a little.

"He sees a rat," Brother James says.

"He finds a lot of them," Daddy says.

We all nod.

I'm watching Rover but now I'm thinking about Buddy. Buddy didn't bother about rats. And he didn't jump on people. He didn't tear around the yard like he was crazy. He barked the squirrels away, and then he laid in the cool of the tree until I came to talk to him. That's what Buddy did. He laid still. And he listened to me.

"I guess," Brother James goes on, "since y'all didn't see

the show, you didn't see about that shelter out in California somewhere."

We shake our heads and keep on watching Rover. I wish he would either catch that rat or leave it alone.

"It's a fine shelter," Brother James says. "Looks like a fancy resort hotel for dogs."

Rover jumps and yelps.

"Just catch it!" I yell at him.

"They showed some of the dogs living there. Some of the ones from Katrina."

I turn to look at him.

He looks at me. "One of those dogs was a black dog—a black dog with three legs."

"Buddy!" I shout, and jump up. "You saw Buddy on TV!"

Brother James grins real big.

"I wanted you to know he's okay, Li'l T. He made it out. He's safe. He's a California dog now, but he's safe."

"Daddy," I say. "Let's go get him."

31

Right away they start making excuses. We don't know what shelter that is. It's too far away. How are we going to get there? Where are we going to get that kind of money?

"But we can find out what shelter it is, can't we, Brother James?" I'm standing right up close to him. I've got his arm in my two hands. I'm shaking it.

"I guess so," he says, kind of laughing. "We could probably call the TV station. Somebody there ought to know."

"How much does it cost to get to California? A hundred dollars?"

They all laugh. "A thousand is more like it," they say.

"For all of us?"

"For one of us," Daddy says. "Slow down, Li'l T." He stands up. "We're not the kind of people who can just pick up and go to California." He stands there kind of quiet for minute. "I'm sorry, son," he says. Then he picks up his hammer and he heads back inside.

•◆•

I can't sleep that night. I'm laying there on my air mattress thinking about Buddy in a cage in California. I'm thinking about how he needs me to tell him stories. How he wants to put his nose in the palm of my hand. I'm wondering what he would think if he knew about Rover. Would he think I forgot him? Would he think I said, "I don't want no piece of a dog. I want me a whole dog"?

I'm thinking we've got money somewhere. Look at that Sheetrock Daddy just piled up in the front room. Look at those shingles he's nailing on the porch roof every day. Where does that stuff come from if we ain't got money?

A thousand dollars. I could earn that much. I could work. Doing odd jobs around. I ain't got no lawn mower anymore but I could do the mowing if somebody had the machine. I could muck out houses. My bicycle's gone, but my legs are strong. I could pick up the trash everywhere. Daddy's going to teach me how to nail Sheetrock. And I know how to saw a board straight. Ain't everybody can do that.

I'm thinking I could even build a new shed with all the

junk wood laying around. I could find an old army blanket just like Granpa T's. I could find new bowls and make a new sign. I could fix it all up almost exactly like it was before.

I'm turning back and forth on my air mattress. It's hot in that house with no fans and no air conditioner. I can hear the crickets in the trees and a car or two on a street somewhere far away. I hear Rover snuffling around under the house and settling in to his sleeping place right below my bed.

And I'm laying there, sweating and doing numbers. How long would it take me to earn a thousand dollars? What could I do to get it?

One more time I'm thinking up a plan. One more time I'm figuring out a way. Because there's one thing I know for sure—I'm going to get that money and I'm going to bring my Buddy home.

•◆•

The next Sunday I go to church with an armload of signs. I stick them up on the bulletin board by the sanctuary. I stick them up on the wall by the Sunday school. I start handing them out to the people as they walk in the door.

Mama shakes her head. Daddy says I'm crazy. I say I want my dog.

BOY FOR HIRE, my sign says. WHAT YOU NEED DONE, I'LL DO IT. That's in big letters. Then it says, "Katrina rescuers took my dog to California. I got to go get him. It costs a thousand dollars to go to California." Then I put a picture of a dog. I drew it just like Buddy—black with three legs. Then under the picture it says, "Please help me get my dog back. Tyrone Elijah Roberts."

When I walk in to sit down, I see people looking at me. Mrs. Washington's nephew nods but he don't smile. Mr. Nelson's grinning. A little white boy stands up on his seat just to get an eyeful. I try to act like I know what I'm doing. I try to act like a boy who can do anything.

After church, I go home and wait for the phone to ring.

The first call comes from Brother James. "The church still has a lawn," he says. "And it's still got a lawn mower."

"When do you want me to come?"

"Saturday. Just like before."

The second call comes from Mrs. Washington's nephew. He says his name is Eddie. He says he's doing that house all by himself. He says sometimes he could use a hand.

"When do you want me to come?"

"I'll be at work tomorrow," he says. "What about the next day?"

A white lady three streets off and around the corner needs somebody to pull out all her dead bushes. She says she's finally tired of looking at them.

I take Rover with me on that one. I figure he's about as good at digging as anybody. I almost fall out laughing when I see those bushes. They're dead as everything else, but that lady took spray paint and sprayed all the leaves green. "It helped for a while," she says, "but it's time to plant new."

Everybody I work for tells me, "Good luck with your dog."

I tell them, "Call me again. And tell your friends to call me, too."

Daddy catches me one night sitting on my mattress counting my money. I've got the battery lamp lit up beside me and I'm putting the fives in one stack, the tens in another, and my single twenty all by itself.

"How much you got?" Daddy says.

"Sixty bucks."

"In one week?"

"Pretty good, huh?" I say.

Daddy nods real slow. "How long is it going to take you to get to a thousand?"

I start doing the math in my head. "Sixteen—seventeen weeks."

Daddy nods again. “About four months.”

We sit and look at the money.

“Buddy was your dog for about four months,” he says.

I look at him again. “What are you saying, Daddy?”

“Nothing,” he says. “I ain’t saying nothing at all.”

•◆•

The second week I earn a hundred bucks and I tell Daddy it’s going to go faster than we thought. He says that’s all well and good for me to be working for other people during the week but on Saturday the only thing I can do is mow at the church. The rest of the day he needs me at the house. The front room is all wired now. It’s time to start hanging that Sheetrock.

Saturday morning when I finish at the church, Brother James comes out with my five dollars and hands me a letter.

“This is some news about Buddy,” he says, and goes on back inside.

I don’t wait to get home to read it. I sit right down on the church steps and unfold the paper. It’s addressed to Brother James.

“Dear Reverend James,” it says. “Thank you for writing to inquire about the black, amputee, mixed-breed dog featured on the recent television documentary. You are correct. The dog you saw is indeed named Buddy, and our records show that he was rescued from a second-floor bathroom in a house in New Orleans. Because he was never claimed, we put him up for adoption. A local family adopted him about six months ago. We do not provide the names of adoptive families but we have passed on your information to them. It is our policy to leave it up to the adoptive family to decide whether to contact prior owners. Thank you very much for your interest. Sincerely," and so on.

I fold up that letter real careful. I sit there a while and look at the sidewalk. I ain't never noticed before how that cement's got little black spots and little gray spots and even little red spots all mixed up in it. I bend down to stare at it, and then I sit up and take out the letter and read it again. Then I remember Daddy's waiting for me at home. I fold up the letter and slide it deep into my pocket. I think maybe I'll wait until the end of the day to show it to Daddy. Or maybe I'll wait until tomorrow.

At home, they're setting up to hang that Sheetrock. Eddie's come over to help. When we get going, I'm sure glad he's there, because hanging Sheetrock is the hardest thing I've ever done. That Sheetrock's heavy as a ton of bricks and there ain't nothing for it but to pick it up sometimes and hold it where you need it. Daddy and Eddie do most of the lifting and Mama and me are trying the best we can to help. By the end of the day, I see Mama can't hardly help no more. She's completely worn out. Daddy tells her to go on and check on Tanya and the baby while we finish up. I hear her barely dragging her feet along the floor while Eddie and me are holding up that last piece and Daddy's banging home those nails. When we're done, we step back and take a look and Daddy says, "Whoo-ee," and I say, "We started. I guess we can finish." And Eddie laughs and goes on outside to start washing up.

Then I pull the letter out of my pocket and hand it to Daddy. "Brother James gave this to me this morning," I say.

Daddy's standing there reading it with his arms all covered in Sheetrock dust and his hair powdered over with white.

He looks up at me. "Why you ain't showed me this before?" he says.

"We were busy," I say.

"So what do you think?" he says.

I shrug.

"Wonder who these people are," he says, and turns over the letter to look on the back.

"Ain't nothing on the back," I say. "That's all there is."

"Buddy's a lucky dog," Daddy says. "He's got a new home."

He gives me back the letter.

I fold it up real careful and shove it in my pocket. "It ain't fair," I say.

"Come on," Daddy says. "Let's get cleaned up."

Outside Eddie's washing himself off with the hose. He starts spraying me and then we're spraying each other and then Daddy gets wet and then even Mama joins in. She's squealing like a little girl and we're shooting water all over her and Tanya. Baby Terrell's sitting in a puddle and splashing his hands.

Rover's hopping all around and trying to bite the water out of the air. Then he goes galloping across the yard and knocks Baby Terrell smack over into the puddle. I snatch up Baby Terrell. He's screaming like he's been shot, but all he is is wet. Rover runs off to the corner of the yard. He sits down and looks at us.

I put down Baby Terrell and I grab up a stick and chase after Rover. "Bad dog!" I'm shouting. "You're a bad dog!" I hit him hard on his behind. He yelps. I smack at him again and he runs off. "I'll get you," I yell, but Rover disappears under the house.

I turn around and Daddy's standing there holding the hose.

"Buddy wouldn't have done that," I say. "Buddy had better sense!"

Daddy walks over to the spigot and turns off the water. He looks at Mama. "Take Tanya and the baby on home," Daddy says. He looks at Eddie. "Thank you," he says. "I guess we're done for the day." Then he looks at me. "Li'l T, come here with me."

Daddy takes me inside. He stands in front of me and crosses his arms over his chest.

I'm standing there with water dripping off me. I'm waiting for him to lift his hand.

"That dog don't have any idea what he did wrong." Daddy waits a minute. "But you do."

I know he's going to hit me now.

But he don't. He just talks. "You're striking out in anger, son. It don't work. It never will."

He heaves up a sigh from deep in his chest, then he leans against the door frame and looks up at the ceiling.

"Buddy ain't your dog no more," he says. "And we can't go to California. I'm sorry. I'm sorry that I'm always saying I'm sorry."

32

I don't think I can go to church the next morning. Eddie's going to be there. He's going to know I'm the kind of boy who would hit a dog like that. He's going to say, "That boy don't deserve to get his dog back from California." And he's going to be right.

But Daddy says I got to go. And Mama says I'm not sick, I'm just lazy. She says if anybody ought to stay in bed it's her, because she can hardly raise up her arms, but one thing she's not doing is missing church.

I get off easy. Eddie ain't in church. I guess he's more worn out than he let on. We're filing out afterward, and three different people come up to me with work they need done. The lady who had all her bushes ripped out wants me to come plant her new ones. Mr. Nelson's decided he wants to do something about his front yard and wants me to come over and start whacking down the weeds so at least he can see what's going on in the street from his front window. An old lady I never noticed before says can I come over and help her move her sofa. She don't like where it is and she can't lift it by herself.

I'm making all my arrangements when Brother James comes up to me. "Got another letter yesterday," he says. "It came after you left out. You'll like this one better."

I grab it out of his hands and huddle off to the side of the steps while he's still shaking hands and Mama and Daddy are chatting up the neighbors.

"Dear Reverend James, We are the family who adopted Buddy. Katrina caused so much loss. It makes us sad to think that a family also lost such a wonderful, kind, dear dog as Buddy. Please put us in touch with the family who lost Buddy. We love Buddy very much, but we want to do the right thing. Perhaps something can be worked out."

I don't even get to the "sincerely" part before I'm jumping up and grabbing Daddy's arm and saying, "Read this! Look here, Daddy! Read this!"

He says what happened to my manners and I say, "Read this. Here. Read it."

So he takes it out of my hands, and he reads it, and then

he passes it over to Mama. She reads it with her forehead all wrinkled up and says, "Well, I'll be." Then she gives it back to Daddy and Daddy gives it back to me.

"Well, Li'l T," he says, "I hope you got some of your Granpa in you. I hope you know how to write a good letter. It's all on you now."

•◆•

I write the best letter that's ever been written in the whole wide world. I tell them the whole story. How I'd been wanting a dog all my life and Daddy always said we didn't have the money and then—*wham*—we ran into Buddy on the way to church and it was meant that he would be my dog. I explain about why we left him and how it didn't turn out like we planned. I tell them about coming to the house and finding the note, all faded and pale. I tell them how we saw Buddy on TV and I'm working to earn money and I hope—oh, how I hope—when I get enough money, I can fly out to California and bring Buddy home.

I work on that letter all day Monday and put it in the mailbox just before Daddy gets home. He comes up the steps to the porch and I'm waiting for him with a copy of what I wrote. He says he don't see how anybody can say no to that letter. He washes off in the hose and pops open a beer from the cooler he keeps in the house, and he sits down to rest. It won't be long before we'll walk over to the widow's house and get some supper with Mama and the rest, but right now we're just going to sit on the porch and stare at the evening.

We ain't been staring five minutes when up comes Mr. Nelson. He's walking fast like he's in a hurry or like he's mad. I'm thinking was I supposed to go there today. Was it today?

He sits down beside Daddy on the step.

"You want a beer?" Daddy says.

He shakes his head. "I don't have time."

"Was I supposed to come today?" I say.

He looks up at me like he's just noticed me. "No, no. Whenever." He waves his hand at me like I ain't hardly there.

Daddy's looking hard at him. "What's troubling you?"

He takes a deep breath. "I got some bad news."

Daddy waits a second but Mr. Nelson don't say anything. "Well, tell it," Daddy says.

Mr. Nelson gives me a sideways glance. "It's about your friend," he says, "that J-Boy."

Daddy raises up his eyebrows.

"And about Eddie," Mr. Nelson says.

Daddy sets down his can.

"Eddie wasn't at church yesterday," I say.

"No," Mr. Nelson says. "He's in jail."

"Jail! What for?" Daddy says.

"He shot J-Boy."

We can't think of one single word to say.

Mr. Nelson's sitting there nodding his head, then he twists to look at me again. "But don't worry," he says real quick. "J-Boy ain't dead."

"How—" I start.

Mr. Nelson holds up his hand. "I'll tell it. I just got to think how to start."

We wait.

"It's like this. Turns out J-Boy's living here by himself. His mama's still in Houston."

"I knew that," I say.

"He ain't got nowhere to live. He's hanging with a bunch of thugs. They're camping out in empty houses."

Daddy looks over at me and I look back at him.

"They're stealing to feed themselves."

"And to buy their drugs," Daddy says.

"That, too," Mr. Nelson says.

"So what's all that got to do with Eddie?" Daddy says.

"Everybody knows Eddie's got guns in that place he's staying. Everybody knows he's over here Saturday helping you hang rock. He gets home Saturday evening and his place has been broke into. It's been tossed up and down. But Eddie ain't no fool. He's got his guns hid in a place he made in the floor. He hears a noise. He gets his gun. He creeps through the rooms. And there's J-Boy, pulling Eddie's clothes out of his drawers and stuffing Eddie's jewelry in his pocket.

"Eddie says, 'Stop!' and J-Boy reaches for something under his shirt.

"Eddie shoots. J-Boy falls. Eddie calls the police. They take J-Boy to the hospital and Eddie to the jail."

"But that ain't fair," I say. "What's Eddie going to do?"

Mr. Nelson heaves a sigh. "Ain't nothing he can do," Mr. Nelson says. "Ain't nothing at all."

•◆•

Wednesday night, we all go to prayer meeting. We don't usually go to that but Brother James is going to pray on Eddie and we want to be there. The church is full. Brother James starts out talking about sorrow and he moves on to strength. When he starts up the praying part, he asks God to forgive Eddie. I ain't sure what Eddie's done that he needs forgiving for but then Brother James says everybody needs forgiveness and he asks God to forgive J-Boy, too.

Then he gets to the "what are we going to do about it" part.

Mr. Nelson said there ain't nothing we can do about it

but Brother James thinks different. He wants us to pray. He wants us to keep Eddie in our prayers every day. He wants us to remember Mrs. Washington and how she was so kind to everybody who crossed her path and how she raised up Eddie when there wasn't anybody else to do the job and how Eddie turned out so good and he went off to Iraq and served his country and how now it's our turn to serve him with our prayers.

Then Brother James changes it up a little.

"But we can do more, Lord," he prays. "Lord, you know that old saying—'God gives every bird its food, but he don't throw it in his nest.' What does that mean? It means you give us the tools, Lord, but we got to pick them up and use them. And what is the tool we've got that's going to help Brother Eddie? Right now, the one thing we've got that we can use is money. Lord, I hate to even mention that word in a prayer. Seems like we get all twisted up sometimes about money. But we've got to remember that money ain't nothing but a tool. It's what we use to get what we need. And right now what Eddie needs is to get out of that jail so he can go on with his work until that trial comes up and that jury finds him innocent of all charges—because we know that's what's going to happen, Lord, in the end. And it ain't right for Eddie to be sitting in that jail until that time comes. Lord, we've got to find a way to bail Eddie out of jail and the only tool we've got to do that with is money.

"So we're praying today, Lord, for you to show us the way to find the money to set our brother free. Amen."

Lots of times when Brother James prays like that, people are shouting out during the prayer or hollering, "Hallelujah!" when it's done. But this Wednesday night, the whole church is sitting there quiet and still. Ain't nobody standing up and saying, "I've got a dollar I can give."

I ain't surprised. Brother James is talking about a lot of money. Ain't nobody sitting there got much to spare. They've got houses to build and babies to feed. Maybe there's somebody else sitting in jail we don't know about. Maybe they've got sorrows they ain't shared.

Brother James is standing there at the front of the church with his hands held up in the air. He's looking out over the congregation. He's waiting for somebody to stand up and give his mite. He's waiting and he's waiting. But nobody stands up.

I poke Daddy. "Ain't you got a dollar?" I whisper.

"If everybody in this room gives one dollar," he whispers, "we won't even make a dent."

Brother James's arms are drifting down. That room is hot as Hades. I'm sweating and shifting in my seat.

All a sudden, I stand up. I can't believe it. My mouth pops open and I hear myself talking. "I've got some money to give," I say. "I've got two hundred and fifteen dollars. I'll give that."

I sit down fast so I don't faint. My heart is beating so loud I can't hear any other sound. Daddy's looking at me like I lost my mind. Mama reaches out her hand and puts it on my knee. Tanya's grinning with her mouthful of white teeth. I hear other people starting to stand up. I hear people singing out numbers. I bend my head down.

Oh, Buddy, I'm thinking. *What have I done? What have I just done?*

33

Daddy says I should be joyful that I'm giving all my money to bring Eddie home instead of Buddy. I don't feel joyful. I feel sad.

The next day, I stack up all my bills on my bed and I count them out. I said wrong at church. I don't have $215. I have $250. I'm sitting there looking at my stacks. I only promised $215. I can keep $35. But then I pick it all up and stuff every last bill in that envelope.

What am I going to keep $35 for? I can't do anything with $35. It ain't going to get me to California one day sooner.

I put that envelope in my pocket and I carry it to the church and I hand it to Brother James.

"Is that your California money?" he says.

I nod.

"Eddie's going to appreciate this."

I nod again.

"You're still doing your jobs around?"

"Yes, sir."

"You got any of your signs left over?"

I point to the church bulletin board.

"Maybe I can drum you up a little more business," he says.

I shrug. "Maybe," I say. "But I'm running out of time."

"You've got your whole life, boy."

"School starts up in two weeks. I have to study. And Daddy says I have to work at our house on the weekends. That don't leave me much time."

Brother James is looking at me. "Your daddy's doing right, son," he says. "School first, and family. That's how you get on in the world."

I nod.

Then Brother James hands me another letter.

"I'm getting to be your post office, boy," he says.

But this letter ain't from California. I start to get a little dizzy. It ain't from Chicago either, but I recognize Jamilla's writing in a second.

"She's looking for you," Brother James says, and goes on back in the church.

I sit myself down on the front steps and hold that letter in my hands. It's clean and flat. She wrote it with a purple pen. It says it's from Virginia.

I reach in and pull out two sheets of paper. The top one is a letter. It says, "Dear Brother James, Do you remember me? I hope so. Chicago was too cold so we left. We're in Virginia now but it's cold, too. We miss New Orleans. We heard about Katrina. We're worried about Li'l T and his family. Where are they? How can I write him a letter? He wrote me about his dog. If you know where he is, please send him this picture."

I look at the second page. It's a drawing of a dog. A black, three-legged dog. Across the bottom, in big, square letters, she wrote, "Li'l T's Dog—Buddy."

I fold up the letter. I fold up the picture. I put them in my pocket.

I sit there a minute until I don't feel so dizzy, then I head home.

When I get back to the house, I start right in to taping Sheetrock. It's a quiet job. You mix up the mud. You smear it on the joints. You press the tape on top and smear on some more mud. When it's dry, you sand it smooth.

It's a job I can do all by myself. Mix, smear, press. Mix, smear, press. After a while, I forget about all the letters. I forget about Eddie. I forget about my money. I keep hoping

I'm going to forget about Buddy, but there ain't enough Sheetrock in the world to make me do that.

•◆•

The rest of that week, I think about writing Jamilla back but I don't do it. I guess she can wait. I did. I don't even tell anybody she wrote. It don't change anything, so what's the use.

On Sunday when I go to church I don't look at anybody as I walk in. I sit in the seat next to Daddy and I stand up when everybody else does and I open my mouth and I sing, but I ain't feeling joyful.

I look over, and Eddie's standing across the aisle and he's singing. He glances over at me and smiles, but I don't smile back. I'm feeling sad. I'm feeling angry.

When we get to the part where Brother James does his long prayer, I wish I had earplugs. I wish I could stick my fingers in my ears and hum.

"First off, Lord," Brother James starts out, "we have so much to thank you for. Brother Eddie is here today because you showed us how to help him. You showed us the true meaning of money, Lord. It's a tool. It's something you use, not something you keep. You helped us help Brother Eddie, and we are eternally grateful."

"Amen," somebody sings out in the back.

I look over at Eddie. His head is bending down and his lips are moving. All a sudden I wonder what it's like sitting in jail. I wonder what it's like thinking about your aunt who raised you up. I wonder if you say a prayer of thanksgiving that she ain't there to see you. I wonder if you just want to shrivel up and die right there. I wonder if you think life just ain't worth living if you're sitting in jail like that.

"The Lord giveth," Brother James goes on, "and the Lord taketh away."

"That's the truth," people say, and I agree with them.

Tanya starts banging her shoes on the chair and Mama pokes her.

"A few Sundays ago, Lord," Brother James says, "this church was papered over with signs."

I look up. Brother James's eyes are shut tight.

"Signs about a dog," Brother James says.

I get all hot.

"Signs about a dog that ain't where he belongs. A dog that's been whisked away to a distant place."

Daddy's beside me, sitting real stiff.

"Signs about a boy who wants that dog home so bad he thinks he can work his way out to California and get him."

Tanya casts her eye at me and grins. "That's you," she mouths.

I purse up my lips like I'm sucking a lemon. I bend down my head.

"Lord, you watched that boy give all his California money to set Brother Eddie free. There you were, Lord, sitting up in your heaven and looking down on us, and you saw him do that and it filled you up with joy."

I'm hotter than I've ever been in my life. I'm thinking I'm going to melt into a puddle right there on that seat.

"Lord, we know you are proud of your child. You are proud of his generosity and his courage and his strength. And so you reached out your hand from on high, and you made a move."

I've got myself tucked low as I can get but I still feel like there's a spotlight shining straight down on me.

"Those signs," Brother James goes on, "didn't stay in this church. They made their way out into the world. People out there saw them. Phone calls were made. Letters were written. Hands were shook.

"Lord, the Bible says the Lord giveth and the Lord taketh away. But maybe they got it backward. Maybe it ought to say the Lord taketh away, and the Lord giveth back. Because you're giving today, Lord. You're giving to that boy who made those signs. Lord, you're the one who touched the people out there in the world who read those signs. You're the one who moved their hearts to generosity. You're the one who gathered them together exactly where they needed to be. And you're the one who, through your almighty power and everlasting grace, has delivered to this congregation on this very morning, two airplane tickets to California leaving on Wednesday."

I can't help it. I pop up out of my chair without thinking. The whole congregation starts cheering. It ain't like a prayer at all. It's like a football game. They're all cheering and clapping. Eddie comes right across the aisle and starts pounding me on the back, and Brother James comes walking down from out of the pulpit with two folded-up pieces of paper in his hand and a grin as wide as the Mississippi River shining on his face.

"God picked you for that dog, son," he says, and he hands the tickets to me. "You fly on out there, and you bring your Buddy home."

34

I ain't never flown on a real airplane before but Daddy did. He says when he was in the army a thousand years ago he flew around to various "garden spots" of the military. He won't talk about any of them. He just nods and says, "Um-hm," and that makes me think about Granpa T saying that exact same thing.

Wednesday morning, we pack up a little suitcase borrowed from the widow. Mama gives us some pralines for the lady in California. She wraps them up in tissue paper and sticks them in a box so they won't break. She says I have to carry them in my hands the whole way. When she walks out the room, Daddy tells me real quiet not to worry. He says we'll put them in the suitcase when we get to the airport. If they get broke, they get broke. I tell Tanya she's going to have

to feed Rover while I'm gone. She says okay and can she dress him up. I give her a look and she don't ask again. We put on the nicest clothes we've got, and Brother James drives us out to the airport.

All the way out there, Brother James is talking nonstop. He's explaining about how he knows somebody who knows somebody who knows a man who flies around in airplanes on his business so much he sometimes gets tickets for free. When that man heard about Buddy, he was falling all over himself to give us those tickets. He says maybe he'll come meet Buddy when we get him home, and Brother James says maybe we'll call the newspaper and they'll do a story. He says we could use a happy story instead of all the sad ones we read all the time. Like about how it was at the airport during the storm when the old, sick people were laying on the floor all scared and tired and confused, and the helicopters were *whomp-whomp*ing in from the hospitals with more and more people, and that lady who wasn't even a nurse had to deliver a baby right out there on the runway in the middle of the afternoon in the scorching heat and sun.

Brother James keeps on talking but I ain't listening to any of that stuff. I've heard enough about Katrina to last my whole life. I'm thinking about California now. I'm thinking I'll see some different stuff out there. I'll see mountains. I'll see the ocean. In some places, they say, you can see them both at the same time.

Then I'm thinking that's all going to be just fine, but the most important thing I'm going to see is Buddy.

Brother James waves us good-bye and we walk through the metal detector and stroll on down that great big old hall like we've been doing this all our lives. They've got that zydeco music playing and they've got a Lucky Dog cart right there inside the building. Daddy says I can get a hot dog if I want. He says we've got plenty enough money for something like that.

Then that plane rolls down the runway and takes off, and I'm thinking, *I'm flying for real.* I'm really up in the sky. I'm really looking down and seeing things with my real eyes.

I can see the swamp spreading out down there all brown and fuzzy with trees. I can see roads like snail tracks shining in the sun. I can see the top sides of the clouds when I ain't never seen nothing before but the bottom sides.

And when I think about why I'm in that airplane and where I'm going and what I'm doing, I can't hardly sit still in that scratchy, old seat.

The flight attendant squats down beside me. "Is this your first time in the air?" she asks, and smiles all pretty.

I nod.

"Don't be scared," she says. "We'll take good care of you."

I laugh. I ain't scared. I'm happier than I've ever been in my whole life.

•◆•

You can't see as much with real flying as I thought. We pass over the deserts. We pass over the mountains. But we can't see any of it. I read the magazine in the pocket in front of me. I eat the food, and it ain't good. I look out the window at enough clouds to last me forever. Just about when I think I'm going to go crazy with clouds, a voice comes over the radio and says we're about to land.

"Praise God," Daddy says, and all a sudden I realize he's been scared the whole way. He's been doing just like Granpa T, pretending he's asleep because he don't like where he is.

"You been scared, Daddy?" I say.

"Course not." He huffs up his shoulders and shivers his head.

I laugh, but he don't think it's one bit funny.

We drag off the plane with everybody else. People are carrying all kinds of stuff. We ain't got nothing but the one suitcase and it's somewhere in the belly of the plane. We're walking slow. We pass out of the hall into the airport.

"What do we do now, Daddy?" I say.

And then I don't wonder. There's a woman and a boy standing not ten feet away. They're holding up a sign. It says, WELCOME, TEE JUNIOR AND LITTLE TEE.

I frown. I ain't "Little Tee." I'm "Li'l T."

Daddy's walking straight over to them. He's holding out his hand. He's shaking hands with the lady and they're talking about the plane ride and the heat and all the people they've got in that great big airport.

That boy and me are just looking at each other.

He's white, just like the woman. He ain't as tall as me but I guess he's about as old. He's got brown hair flopping around in girly curls. He's wearing something that looks like a bathing suit and a T-shirt with a surfboard on it. He's got on flip-flops.

I'm standing there in my Sunday best and feeling like a fool, so I hold out my hand. "I'm Li'l T," I say. Then I can't help myself. "Not Little Tee. Li'l T."

He takes my hand. "I'm Brian," he says.

We pump once and let go. Then we look away.

"Thank you," Daddy's saying. "Come on, son." He and the white lady are walking off talking a mile a minute. Brian and me follow, but we don't say anything.

After we get our suitcase, that lady puts us in the car and drives us out into the city. It's night but I can tell California don't look anything like New Orleans. I don't see any columns on any of the houses. There ain't no iron fences. There ain't no big old live oak trees.

Once we get into the mountains, it's pitch-black dark, just like Mississippi. Then we go over a big hill and there are lights spread out everywhere in front of us. We go around a curve, and it's all dark again.

Daddy and the lady are sitting in the front seat talking away but Brian and I don't say anything.

We drive and drive and drive.

We get to a little town and then we pull in the driveway of a house. It's a new house. It's got a wide driveway and a tall wood fence around the backyard.

"Buddy's here?" I say to Brian.

He nods.

I feel my heart going like a race car.

We walk inside. She flips on the light and drops her keys on a glass table. They make a loud rattling noise and then I hear a *click, click, click* somewhere on the tile floor in that house.

I'm standing there with my hand resting on that glass table top and part of my mind is saying, *Take your hand off. You'll make a spot.* But I don't move. I'm looking down the hall.

And then there he comes.

He's a shadow in a hall of shadows. He gets into the light and then he stops. He's standing there looking at us and I'm looking at him. I notice two things. He's got a fake, metal leg stuck on his stump and his tail is curved up, but it ain't wagging.

"Hello, Buddy," the woman says.

She stoops down and Buddy comes trotting into the room. "You remember Little Tee," she says, "and his daddy."

"Li'l T," I say. I walk over and hold out my hand. Buddy lays his nose in the palm of my hand. His tail starts thumping. He looks up at me with his big old eyes and there's his caterpillar eyebrow, still sticking out like crazy on his forehead.

"He remembers me," I say. I look up at all those people and I smile. "Of course he remembers me," I say. "He's my dog."

Brian spins around all a sudden and walks out the room. I hear a door slam down the hall.

"I'm sorry," the lady says.

But I ain't listening. I'm watching Buddy clicking down that hallway, following after Brian as fast as he can.

35

The next morning the lady says we've only got one day in California, and she's going to show us a good time. She says we're going back over the mountains to the beach because I ain't never seen the ocean before. She says nobody's quite lived until they've seen the ocean. I feel like I've done plenty of living already, but I don't say nothing. We all pile in the car. This time, Buddy's sitting on the backseat right smack between me and Brian.

We ain't hardly got started when we pass a school.

"That's Brian's school," the lady says.

It looks like a school on TV.

"You're close enough to ride your bike," I say.

"I don't ride a bike."

"You ain't got one?"

He cuts his eyes at me. "I didn't say that," he says. "I said I don't ride one."

I shrug my shoulders and look out the window again. Now I can really see the mountains. They are giant hills with dry, brown grass growing on them. In some places you can see where the dirt just fell off the side of the mountain and piled up a couple of hundred feet below. Sometimes there are great big old rocks sticking out of the dirt or perched up on top of a cliff. Sometimes there's a cactus hanging on the side of the hill, just like in the movies.

"Are those mountains ever green?" I ask Brian.

He swivels his face toward me. "When it rains," he says.

"How long has it been since it rained?"

He looks like he's thinking. Then he shrugs. "Three, maybe four months."

I can't believe it. "In New Orleans, it rains almost every afternoon in the summer."

He don't say nothing. He puts his hand on Buddy's head. Buddy shifts a little and puts his head in Brian's lap. Brian turns and looks out the window.

We keep on riding.

Finally we're down out of the mountains and in the city. Eventually we park on a street where there are all kinds of little stores selling stuff that looks like it was made for ladies. Daddy gives me some spending money and I buy a hair bow for Tanya and a soap that's shaped like a shell for Mama.

The lady says, "You're so thoughtful."

I say, "You try going all the way to California and not bringing them back something."

Daddy's standing over in the corner and he starts tee-heeing, and I say, "Where is that ocean anyway?"

We walk out of the store and down the street, and at the end of it—*boom*—there's the ocean. We step on a walkway made out of boards up near the street. People are everywhere. Then there's about a mile of sand before you get to the water. Then the land just stops and there ain't nothing but water, as far as you can see, and those great big old waves rolling in and crashing on the people swimming. I'm standing there all amazed and Daddy's um-hmming beside me when Buddy takes off running across the sand. And then I'm even more amazed. I ain't never seen him run before. Not once.

Brian goes running after him. They're chasing up and down.

The lady says, "Little Tee, why don't you go with them."

So I step off the walkway into the sand. I walk and walk and walk. They're running back and forth. Brian pulls a ball out of his pocket and throws it a long way. Off Buddy goes, racing after it. He brings it back to Brian and Brian throws it again.

Finally I get all the way down to them. Brian's squatting down and rubbing Buddy's neck. He looks up at me.

"When Buddy first got here," he says, "he was afraid of the water." Brian stands up and throws the ball. Buddy goes flying after it.

"He just laid down in the sand when we came to the beach," Brian says. "And look at him now. He loves it."

"It's the sound," I say. "That ocean's so loud."

"Loud?" Brian says.

I nod.

Brian turns and looks toward the water. "I never thought of that," he says. "It just sounds like ocean to me."

"It sounds like roaring," I say. "It sounds like a hurricane."

Buddy's back with the ball. Brian takes it out of his mouth. It's all slobbery. "You throw it," Brian says.

I swing back and throw that ball way off down the beach. Buddy's running after it before my arm even starts going down.

Brian's standing there looking after him. The wind's blowing his girly curls all around his head. He's smiling.

"We ain't got a beach like this in New Orleans," I say,

"but when I get Buddy home, we can go to the park to throw the ball. Or maybe Mama will let me go all the way to the levee now."

Brian turns around and looks at me. He ain't smiling no more. Buddy comes up carrying the ball. I reach out my hand. Brian reaches out his hand, too. Buddy stops. He's standing there looking at us, his eyes going back and forth between us. He's panting. Slobber's drooling off the ball. Those two hands stay stuck out toward him. Buddy dips his head like he's about to drop the ball, but he don't.

Then all a sudden Brian turns around and walks off. Buddy watches him, then he gives me the ball.

I throw it long and hard.

And I can't help it. I'm the one who's smiling now.

•◆•

After a while, I start to get cold on that beach. Buddy's doing all that running and he's got fur, so he's okay. But here I am in the middle of the day in August standing on a beach, and I'm cold. I look up and the others are all huddled up, too, watching Buddy and me playing with the ball. I throw it one last time. When he comes trotting back with it, I take it and kneel down in front of him to rub him up all around his ears and down his neck.

"So you like that?" I'm saying. "You like chasing that ball? You like running on this beach?"

Buddy's panting and panting with his tongue hanging out, his ears pricked up, and his tail standing high like he's ready to go for the ball again anytime I'm ready to throw it.

I feel his collar and dig it out from under his fur. It's a new one but it's still red. The tag says "Buddy" on it, and it's got Brian's name and phone number, too.

"So Brian's afraid you'll run off," I say. "Have you been thinking about running off?"

Buddy don't say nothing. He just sits down on the sand, looking me in the eye and listening so hard his ears twitch.

I hold his face between my hands and rub under his ears with my fingertips. "You were thinking about coming to find me, weren't you?" I say. "Like those dogs do in the movies. All the way across the mountains."

Buddy still don't say nothing but he keeps looking straight at me with his big old brown eyes, just as soft as always.

I'm thinking he wishes he could tell me all about it. All about how he was going to jump out the window of that California house. How he was going to cross the mountains and trot along the side of the road for weeks and weeks. How one day he was going to come down our street and then there I'd be, waiting for him just like he'd always waited for me.

"That would be a fool thing to do, Buddy," I said. "I'm glad you didn't try."

I'm rubbing the top of his head. I'm stretching his eyes way open like Granpa T used to do and that caterpillar eyebrow is climbing up his forehead. I let go and it eases back down where it belongs.

"Or maybe," I say real soft, "maybe you weren't thinking about coming back to me at all. Maybe you're mad at me because I left you behind."

I can see in Buddy's eyes he remembers that bathroom.

"Were you scared," I say, "when that storm came and there wasn't nobody there but you?"

Buddy dips his head and whines a little bit.

"They made me do it," I say. "Daddy and Mama and Granpa T."

Buddy lifts up his white paw and pats me on the knee.

"I was going to stay," I say. "I was going to make soup for Mrs. Washington. I was going to—Buddy, she—"

Then I'm wrapping my arms around his neck and rubbing my face in his soft, soft fur. I'm smelling his old, leaf smell, and I'm feeling his cold nose snuffling in my ear. His warm breath is puffing on my eyelids and his wet tongue is licking me all over my face.

"I'm sorry, Buddy," I'm saying, over and over again. "I am so, so sorry."

•◆•

When Buddy and I get back to the boardwalk, the others are already walking ahead to the car. We follow them, and Buddy trots along beside me just like we're headed off to mow somebody's yard. I'm wondering what he's going to think when he sees the yards in New Orleans now. I'm wondering if he's going to think I've turned lazy since I ain't mowing regular anymore.

At the car, Brian's mama makes us stand in groups for pictures. She arranges us different ways for a while and then Daddy takes some so she can be in them, and finally some stranger takes a couple so we can all be in one together. I can't believe Buddy puts up with all that picture taking, but Granpa T said Buddy had the patience of Job, and I guess he was right.

Then Brian is poking around in the trunk. He comes up with a brush and some cloths and starts cleaning up Buddy. Buddy stands there as still as he can while Brian brushes all the sand out of his fur.

Daddy and the lady are watching.

"You take good care of that dog," Daddy says.

"Yes, sir," Brian says.

"I'll do that," I say, and Brian hands over the brush.

Buddy's fur is looking shiny. It's looking black as night. His ribs are all hid. It feels good running that brush over him.

Then Brian wipes Buddy's paws with the cloth. He rubs ointment on the bottom of his feet. Buddy stands still as a statue, lifting up one foot at a time. You can tell he's used to it now.

When he's done wiping, Brian unbuckles Buddy's spare leg.

"Why do you take off his leg?" I say.

"Sand gets under it," Brian says. "We've got to be careful." He cleans real good where it rubs against his skin. He helps Buddy into the car. "He won't need it for the ride. We'll wash it off at home then put it back on."

"You do this every time?"

Brian nods.

"Will you teach me what to do?"

Brian looks at me for a minute. He looks at his mama. She's watching us hard. He looks back at me.

"Of course," he says. "He's your dog."

•◆•

When we get home, Brian goes straight on back to his room. The lady offers us a cold drink and I'm thirsty so I say, "Yes, please."

I'm standing there in the kitchen while she's fishing in the refrigerator. I see Mama's box of pralines is sitting on the counter and somebody's taken a nibble out of one. I don't see how anybody could take one nibble and then stop.

All a sudden, I look over in the corner and there's a big old tray with two bowls. One's got water. One's empty. Both say BUDDY on them. Somebody painted them special.

The lady stands up and hands me a cold drink. She hands Daddy a beer.

"Look at those bowls, Daddy," I say.

Daddy looks at the bowls, too. He looks at me. He looks at the lady. "You've done a lot for Buddy," he says.

"He's a special dog," she says.

"Did you get him that new leg yourself?" Daddy says.

She nods. "Brian insisted."

"All those homeless dogs," Daddy says. "Why did you choose Buddy?"

"Brian loved him."

All a sudden, I don't want my cold drink. I set it down on the counter and push it away. I walk down the hall toward our room. Buddy's laying on the floor by a shut door. His tail thumps as I pass but he don't get up. I go in my room and close the door.

It's a long time before Daddy knocks. It's already getting dark.

"Did that trip wear you out?" he says.

"I guess."

He sits down on the edge of the bed.

"She's firing up the grill," he says. "She's cooking us a steak."

I don't say nothing.

"What's the matter, son?"

I turn over and look at him. "Brian loves Buddy," I say.

Daddy looks out the skinny, little window to one side of the room. "What did you expect, Li'l T?" he says.

"But Buddy's my dog," I say. "Brian can't love him." I turn back over and put the pillow over my head.

"He can love him, and he does," Daddy says. "I don't see what you're so surprised about. It said so right in that letter. Did you think they were lying when they wrote that part?"

I just lay there breathing into my pillow. I can smell the grill in the backyard. I can hear the lady chopping something in the kitchen.

After a while, the mattress jiggles when Daddy stands up.

Then I turn over and look at him. "But Daddy," I say, "do you think Buddy loves him back?"

Daddy don't say nothing. He just turns around and walks out the door.

36

The room gets darker and darker. I hear Buddy clicking around on the tile floor. I hear that sliding door off the back go *whush* when it opens and closes. I wonder why there ain't no ceiling fans, hot as it is.

Then Daddy knocks on the door and comes in again. "Get up," he says. "We're eating."

"I ain't hungry."

"You're eating anyway," he says. "Wash your hands. Then come out here and act like you know how to behave."

Daddy shuts the door and I lay there a minute.

What if I don't? I think. What if I open the door a tiny crack and call Buddy real soft and he comes running and sliding down the hall to me? What if I pull him into the room and tell him, "Sh, sh," and his tail is thumping away while

I'm rubbing the sides of his head and scratching up under his chin? What if I open that skinny, little window and climb out and take Buddy with me and we sneak around the house while they're all standing in the back around the grill? And then we sneak down that curvy street to the road where that side of the mountain is all caved in? And we keep climbing until we get to some woods? And then we—

I tell my head to shut up. That's crazy thinking. What am I going to do all by myself in the woods of California with a three-legged dog? What is my daddy going to do when he finds me gone? What is my mama going to say when he calls her on the telephone?

I'm standing in front of the mirror. I stare at myself. I wash my hands and I go outside.

•◆•

That lady knows how to cook a steak. We eat that steak and a salad all full of tomatoes and some other stuff I ain't never heard of. The whole time we're eating, Daddy's telling her about Katrina and New Orleans. She wants to know everything. She wants to know where we went and what the storm sounded like and what color the water was when we tried to get home. She listens so quiet while Daddy tells about the first time we got back to the house. He tells about the *X* painted on the front and how we went up the stairs and what the bathroom looked like and how there was a note but it was so faded we couldn't read it. She don't move when Daddy tells about how we got home and Granpa T passed that very night.

After Daddy tells it all, we sit quiet for a while and look up at the sky. That sky is big in California. There ain't no trees or tall houses where she lives. You lay on your back on the grass in their yard and you look up and all you see is sky. Sky and stars.

Before long, they all go inside and I'm still laying there looking up. I'm getting cold even though it's summer but I don't want to get up. Then Buddy comes wandering over just like before. He lays down beside me and puts his head on my stomach just like he used to do in the shed.

I put my hand on the top of his head and smooth back his fur. His tail goes *thump*.

"The shed is gone," I tell him. "When we get back, you'll see it's just a heap of wood laying in the corner of the yard."

His tail goes *thump, thump*, and I keep talking. "And that bathroom. Buddy, you sure tore up that bathroom. It don't matter, though, because we had to rip it all out anyway. The water got up under the tile. All the floorboards were starting to rot.

"So I don't have to repaint that door after all. I'm going

to have to paint the brand-new door instead. When we get it. We're about to finish Mama and Daddy's room. Then we're going to do the bathroom. When we've got the bathroom finished, the rest of them are going to move in with me and Daddy. We'll all be together again.

"And you'll be there, too, Buddy. It'll be just like before. Just exactly like before.

"Almost."

I'm looking up at the sky. It's as black as Buddy's fur and full of stars.

"Granpa T passed, Buddy. Did you hear Daddy saying about that? We were all sitting there in the living room of that little apartment talking about his house, and he passed, just like that. We didn't even notice. How long do you suppose he was gone before any of us even looked his way?"

I rub Buddy's ears and he shifts his head on my stomach.

"I'm thinking he went to his place and when it came time for him to come on back, he just said, 'No.' He just said, 'I ain't doing it. I'm too tired.' He ain't never going to say you're ugly again, Buddy. He ain't never going to say you stink."

I stare up at those stars for a while. Then I go on. "So I'm getting his room. My own room. When that room's done, you can sleep with me. I'll tell Mama she has to let you. I'll tell her there ain't no shed anymore and you got used to sleeping inside at this house here in California. I'll tell her that's what you've got to have now.

"And we've got to keep you away from Baby Terrell. He's walking all over the place now, and he's learned how to hit things. He whacked me with his toy train just the other day. I've still got a sore place on my head.

"And Tanya," I say. "I bet you miss her singing. She's learning lots of words now so she's getting better. People say she sings like a bird. She liked singing to you, Buddy. You listened. You ain't like Rover."

And then I stop.

I don't know what to tell Buddy about Rover. I think about it while I look at the stars.

"I've got to explain about Rover," I say. "He ain't a grown-up dog like you. He ain't got no sense. He runs all over the place. He jumps on people. He's got short hair and it's white and brown. He likes to catch rats. I'm teaching him not to put them on the porch. And we're working on the jumping-on-people part. When he learns—"

I stop again. I need to think some more.

"I didn't ask for Rover," I finally explain to Buddy. "Santa Claus brought him. It wasn't part of any plan. Not like with you. You were meant to be my dog, Buddy."

I bend my eyes down toward his face.

All I can see in the dark is his eyes, shining back at me.

"It was meant to be, wasn't it, Buddy?" I say to him, and his tail goes *thump.*

•◆•

When it's late, the lady says it's time for bed. She says our plane don't leave until the afternoon but there are all kinds of things we've got to do to get Buddy ready for his trip.

We go inside the dark house and Buddy goes *click-click*ing down the hall. I'm thinking he's going to the bed in our room now, but he goes in Brian's room instead.

I follow him. Brian's already sitting on his bed. He helps Buddy up. Buddy curls up on one side. Brian looks up and sees me.

"Does he sleep with you every night?" I say.

Brian nods.

"What about that big old dog bed?"

Brian shrugs. "He likes my bed better."

I watch Buddy shift his head a little on his paws. Brian reaches out a hand and smooths Buddy's head. Then he turns and looks at me, "I would never leave Buddy," he says. "Never. No matter what. I would die first."

I spin around and go in our room and slam the door.

•◆•

That's the longest night I ever lived in my life. I can't go to sleep for thinking. I want to go in Brian's room and smack his face. I want to sneak out the door and disappear. When I finally go to sleep, all I can dream about is Buddy in that room snuggled up against that white boy who stole my dog.

Daddy shakes me awake before light. He says to wake up. There's a problem. He don't move off my bed. He sits there listening. I'm listening, too. The sounds in the house ain't right. Somebody's choking. There's a bang on the floor and then Buddy's paws going *click, click, click* down the hall.

Daddy stands up and opens the door real quiet. He's peering this way and that. Then the lady's bedroom door slams back and she comes tearing down the hall and whips into Brian's room with Buddy limping behind her.

"Brian!" she's saying. "Brian!"

Then me and Daddy are both running down the hall.

Brian's laying on his bed with his arms and legs jerking and his eyes rolled up in his head.

"Sweet Jesus," Daddy says.

"It's a seizure," the lady says real fast. "He gets them. Buddy tells me."

She sits down beside him. She's singing at him like he's a baby. "It's okay now," she's singing. "Mommy's here, sweetheart. It's okay."

Brian keeps on jerking. He whams his hand on the headboard. She grabs it and wipes the blood off. She's pushing the covers out of his way so he don't get tangled in them.

"Shouldn't we call the doctor?" Daddy says.

"No," she says. "He'll be okay. This happens."

I look and there's Buddy, standing by the bed watching Brian jerk. Buddy's whining a little bit. He's poking his nose at Brian's foot where it's hanging off the bed.

"Good dog," the lady says.

And then Brian's still. He turns his eyes to his mama like he's exhausted. "It's okay," she says. "Go on to sleep now. You're fine."

She helps Buddy climb back up on the bed and he snuggles up next to Brian. He licks Brian's face and rests his head on Brian's stomach. Brian puts his hand on Buddy's back and closes his eyes. Buddy looks up at us and blinks.

The lady stands up and we all go out. She shuts off the light.

"He'll sleep now," she says. She looks at Daddy and tries to smile. "Good night. Thank you."

Me and Daddy go back in our room. We climb back in our beds. We lay there in the dark waiting for the light.

37

When I wake up again, Daddy's standing next to me all showered and dressed.

"Get up, sleepyhead," he says. "This is your big day."

When Daddy leaves out, I go and look out that skinny window. That California grass just ain't green enough. And those trees ain't much more than bushes. And all the stuff growing up next to the house looks spiky and mean.

I go out to the family room and they're all sitting out on the patio drinking orange juice and eating cantaloupe. When I whush open that sliding door, Buddy lifts up his head and thumps his tail.

"Look at that," Daddy says. "He's looking forward to going home."

I sit down next to Brian. He's got a bandage on his hand where he whacked it on the headboard. He don't look at me.

I can't eat any cantaloupe. I can't drink any juice.

"How about some toast?" the lady says. Her mouth is full of teeth just like Tanya's, and it's smiling. But her eyes ain't smiling.

"No thank you, ma'am," I say, polite as I know how. "I guess I'm just not hungry."

"It's an exciting day," she says, and grins her fakey-looking grin.

•◆•

The lady's still all bright and smiley while we pack our things in the car and get Buddy to climb in the pen in the backseat. She's talking and talking and we're getting in the car and I notice Brian ain't getting in with us.

He's just standing there by the front door with his hands shoved down in his pockets, staring off at the mountains in the distance.

When we're all packed up she says, "Okay, sweetheart. Go on now."

He looks at her almost like he hates her. Then he stomps across the yard to the neighbor's house. He's standing there ringing the bell while we're shutting the car doors. He goes inside just as we pull out of the drive.

The lady's holding on to that steering wheel like she's afraid it's going to fly out of her hands. She's staring at the road and blinking hard. She reaches over and snaps on the radio. Daddy and me both know better than to talk.

We're going back down that twisty-turny road. We're passing the fallen-in mountain. We're passing those old, dry cactuses hanging on the side of the hill.

Then we're turning onto the superhighway with about a million other cars. That radio keeps on playing, one song after the other.

I stick my hand in Buddy's cage and he rests his head in the palm of my hand.

"Does he have those fits much?" I whisper to Buddy, but Buddy don't say anything. "Is that why he don't ride a bicycle?" I say real quiet. Then I lean down close as I can get to Buddy's ear. I smell his smell. "Where do you suppose Brian's daddy is?"

Buddy starts up whimpering. I reach through the wire of the pen and I scratch behind his ears. I rub his skin back on the top of his head and make his eyes stretch open. He keeps poking his nose at my leg and every once in a while he whimpers some more.

It takes a long time to get to the airport. The closer we get, the more cars it seems are on the road. The lady drives in a parking garage and we go around and around so much I start to feel sick.

Finally, she pulls in a space and the car stops moving. We can't carry Buddy in his pen, so we take him out on a leash and Daddy starts to wrestle the pen out of the backseat while the lady drags our suitcase out of the trunk.

I'm holding Buddy on his leash and he's sitting there whining and poking his nose at my feet.

"He must be nervous," the lady says. Her face looks like she got ten years older just on that drive. "It's natural, though," she says. She sets down the suitcase and starts digging in her purse. "I have some medicine for when—"

"I changed my mind," I say.

She stops talking and Daddy stops wrestling. He straightens up out of the car door.

"Say what?" he says.

I swallow big before I open my mouth again. "I say I changed my mind."

"About what?" he says.

"About Buddy," I say.

Daddy and the lady are both staring at me.

I suck in a real deep breath and close my eyes. When I open them, I look up at the sky, but all I can see is roof.

It's all on me.

I start over. "I guess," I say, "Buddy better stay here."

The lady's face goes limp. She looks off into the garage like she's worried about a car coming around the corner but there ain't no traffic in there.

Daddy looks at me hard. "That man gave us his tickets so we could come out here, son. All those people helped. It's a little late to change your mind."

"I know. But this is just what I got to do, Daddy." I look down at Buddy. He's whining and pushing his nose at my feet. "Brother James told me I was the instrument of God," I say. "He said our car hit Buddy so we could save him. I thought I was saving him for me."

I look up at Daddy. He's got his hand over his eyes.

"Turns out," I say, "I was saving him for Brian. I guess that was the plan all along. I just didn't see it."

The lady's got her back to us now. Her shoulders are all curved over. She's leaning one hand on the car next to us.

"Daddy, do you think that man's going to want me to pay him back for those tickets?"

Then the lady turns around and finally speaks up. "No," she says. "Buddy goes back with you. He's your dog. We don't have the right to keep him."

I hand the lady the leash, then I squat down and hold Buddy's head in my hands. I smell that old leaf smell. I rub my finger on his caterpillar eyebrow. He looks at me with his big old brown eyes. "Granpa T says comes a time when you've got to let go," I tell him. "I'm letting go now, Buddy."

I lean my head on top of his and he sticks up his tongue and licks my chin.

"I love you, Buddy," I say. "Good-bye."

Then I can't help it. I start running.

I'm running fast as I can. Daddy grabs up the suitcase and comes chasing after me.

"Li'l T," he's yelling. "Li'l T, stop!"

But I can't stop. I can't look back. I don't want to change my mind.

Then I'm deep in the airport and there's thousands of people all around me and I stop running. I stand there and wait for Daddy. When he catches me up, he puts his arms around me, and I press my face against his chest, and we stand still.

•◆•

I guess even Granpa T couldn't drag this story out much more after that.

We get on the airplane and we take off. Daddy and I don't hardly talk. I'm staring out the window with my teeth all clenched together. He's mad at me and he's not mad at me.

He's pretending like he's asleep one minute then he's looking over at me the next.

When we get home, Tanya busts out crying and that don't help. Mama squinches up her mouth. Brother James shakes his head but I promise to mow at the church for free. And turns out, that man ain't worried a bit about those tickets.

I write Jamilla a long, long letter about everything. I stick two pictures in the envelope. One is from California. The other is one Mr. Nelson took of our whole family sitting on the front steps of our house. It's a good picture because everybody's behaving, even Rover.

Two weeks into school, we finish up the bathroom and we all move in together again. I get some glasses and find out most other people have always been able to see separate leaves on the trees. When Eddie comes over to help us hang the rock in my new bedroom, he says I look like I finally got some sense. Daddy says that would take more than glasses. Tanya says she wants glasses. Mama says is somebody going to nail up this rock or she going to have to hold it there until her arms fall off.

On my fourteenth birthday, I get a card all the way from Virginia and another one from California. Mama and Daddy give me a red bicycle. I ride to the levee with a new boy from my class at school and we throw the ball for Rover all afternoon long.

One Sunday on the way to church, Tanya's playing the fool with Baby Terrell, trying to teach him to sing "Eensy Weensy Spider." Daddy's saying, "Can't y'all be quiet for just one minute?"

And then we look and see the Tomato Man has finally come back. We're passing by him, waving like we're crazy, and all a sudden I stop waving and I say, "Right there. That's where we found Buddy. Right in the middle of St. Roch Avenue."

Mama turns around and looks at me. "I'm sorry, son," she says.

But I'm not sorry. I'm thinking, *This is happiness. This is home.*

ACKNOWLEDGMENTS

My thanks go to Don K. Haycraft, Kendra Levin, Emily Sylvan Kim, and Carole Fulton D.V.M. for the gift of their unflagging support and expertise as Li'l T devised his plan for Buddy, never imagining how Katrina would change his life and life would change his plans.

Turn the page for a sample of
M. H. Herlong's suspenseful
debut novel . . .

GERRY SAYS HE remembers the sun and the fish. All the fish. The silver ones swimming around the rudder at anchor. The brilliant blue ones flashing across the fiery red coral. The big black ones curving like shadows at our bow as we sailed with the Gulf Stream.

But the one he remembers best, he says, is the first one he stabbed with his spear. He tells how he shoved the spear down right into the flounder's head, how he pulled the still-struggling fish from the water, and how he laughed—because he was six years old and could kill a fish.

He remembers all that, he says, but nothing more. He says he was too little when it happened. He says I have to tell him stories.

So I do.

Once upon a time there was family. Then a boat. And then islands.

Once upon a time three boys were lost at sea. One almost drowned. One almost went crazy. One fell off a cliff.

Gerry says I'm making it up, but I'm not. Everything I tell him is the truth. I just don't tell him everything.

I don't tell about the morning we woke up and Dad was gone. I don't talk about the storm. Or when we wrecked on the coral reef. I don't talk about—I never will talk about—when I left Gerry alone, standing there on the empty beach of that desert island with Dylan dying at his feet.

I don't tell stories about those things and I don't need to. Because Gerry is lying. He remembers it all. Sometimes when we go sailing now we watch the shore slip by and we remember together. Not with words or even looks but with blood rhythm—with the rush of electricity from one body to another. I pull in the mainsheet. I lean on the tiller. I tighten the jib. The boat flies.

And I don't need to tell stories. I sit close to my brothers on the rail and I get dizzy. Like when you stump your toe and it hurts so bad you think you'll faint. The world spins backwards. I lose my place in my life. I'm running and I don't know if I'll make it in time. Then it's all starting over again. And it's not a story at all. It's real and I am fifteen.

THE BOAT

CHAPTER ONE

WE DROVE ALL night to get to the boat. I kept asking Dad to stop and let us sleep, but he always said, "No, I want to get a little farther," until Gerry fell asleep leaning against the door, his mouth open and drooling, and Dylan tilted over sideways on the backseat. Somewhere south of Miami, we pulled over at an all-night gas station.

"Dad, please," I said when we got back in the car.

"It's too late," he said, and drove us back onto the dark highway.

So I just sat there for hours, watching us rush into the hot, muggy June night and thinking about the spiky palm trees and mosquitoes and strange, quick lizards scuttling off into the crumbling asphalt along the edge of the road. When we finally made the Keys, my head was aching and the sun was just rising behind us.

"Look." It was Dylan's voice. "The morning star."

I looked. Dylan was barely eleven, but he knew about stars. One star hung there in the sky, still bright enough to be seen in the first light of morning.

"It's Venus," Dylan said.

I closed my eyes, waiting for Dad to start some story or recite some poem, but he didn't. He didn't say anything. Even the way he looked had completely changed. He had wrinkles around his eyes. The gray in his hair shone in the dim morning light.

I shifted in my seat to see Dylan. "It's not a star," I said. "It's a planet."

Gerry stirred in the backseat. "It *is* a star," he said, wiping his face with Blankie.

"You're only five," I said, turning back around in my seat. "What do you know?"

"Dylan says it's a star," Gerry said firmly. "And Dylan knows better than you."

"Be quiet," Dad said. "All of you."

I pressed my forehead against the cool glass of the car window and stared out at the gray ocean. I still couldn't believe it. One day he had just announced we were going sailing for a year. A whole year. "Like on the lake, Ben," he had said. "You'll love it."

"I won't love it."

"But you love sailing."

"I want a car. Mom said I could get a car when I turned sixteen. Five months and I'm supposed to get a car."

"That's not important anymore."

"It *is* important. She said—"

"Enough," he'd said. "Just stop."

I had stopped. What difference did it make what I said? He had already decided.

In Key West, Dad found us a room in a motel near the marina where the boat was docked. Gerry curled up on one bed, holding Blankie bunched in front of his face. I stretched out next to him. Dylan made a pallet on the floor. Dad had the second bed all to himself. I lay watching his still profile backlit through the curtains. Suddenly he sat up trembling and covered his eyes. Then he stood, wiped his face with his shirt-tail, and picked his way through the litter on the floor to step outside and close the door quietly behind him.

I eased out of bed and opened the curtain a tiny bit to look out. Our window faced the parking lot, but I could see a scrap of the marina if I pressed my cheek against the glass. Dad was right. I did love to sail. He and I had explored the lake together for hours, just the two of us. By the time I was twelve, he had let me go out alone on the twenty-two-footer we kept on the lake. For the last year, I didn't even have to ask. I knew all the coves in the lake. I knew the shallows and the deep trench running through the middle. I loved to sail. But I also loved to come home, and this time we weren't coming home.

I climbed back into the bed, but I couldn't sleep. Maybe it was the way Dylan slept so soundly, not moving at all. Or maybe it was the little sniffing, crying noises Gerry was making. He had dropped Blankie on the floor, and his thin, careful fingers were searching for it in his sleep. As I reached to pick it up, he suddenly rose up on his knees, his hair sweaty, his eyes wide open.

"Mom?" he called. *"Mom?"*

I sat up in front of him, but he looked through me.

"Mom!" His voice went shrill. "Mom!"

I touched Blankie lightly to his face. "Gerry," I said, "wake up."

He turned slightly and saw me. His face crumpled. He took Blankie.

"Ben," he whispered. Then he flopped over and curled into a ball facing the wall.

"Are you okay?" I asked.

He jerked his head in a quick nod and covered his face with Blankie.

I looked up and there was Dad, standing halfway in the door.

"He was crying again?" Dad asked.

I didn't say anything. I just lay down beside Gerry and shut my eyes. After a minute or two, Dad left. I wished I could shut my ears too. Why did I have to hear every sound? The maid's cart scraping from room to room. Cartoons on the TV next door. Gerry still whimpering a little. And Dylan so utterly quiet.

I felt as if I hadn't slept in months, as if I had lain in my bed every night, my mind filling up with things while I stared at the stars Dylan and Mom had stuck on the ceiling of our room two summers ago. If I was lucky, my mind would eventually start playing the tapes of a story I liked to tell myself, like the one about the car I was going to get. If I was not lucky, my mind would start playing the other tapes.

In that motel room, my mind started playing the other tapes—over and over. And the first scene was always the same. My mind saw the phone just before it was going to ring. It was lying beside Dad on the sofa, white against the dark blue. I knew it was going to ring, and I couldn't stop it.

It was April, early afternoon, and Dad and I were watching the ball game together on TV. Our team was ahead, but the game was slow and I felt sleepy. Gerry had already fallen asleep on the sofa, his hair still damp from his swimming lesson. Dylan was upstairs. His birthday was next month and he was studying telescope catalogs. At least that's what he told me later.

Mom had left in the car about twenty minutes before to get ice cream.

Then the phone rang.

Sometimes when you read a book or watch a TV show, you see the people and you think, *Don't do that. Don't open that door. Don't answer that phone.* You know everything is about to change. "Stop!" you want to say. "Rewrite the story. Rewind the tape. Don't let it happen that way." But you can't. The people always open the door or answer the phone. The bad thing always happens, and there is nothing you can do about it.

So Dad answered the phone.

"Yes?" he said. Then, "Yes," again. "Oh, my God." A longer pause. "Of course. Right away."

He put the phone down.

Everything had changed and there was nothing we could do about it.

Two blocks away, a guy had run a red light. He had killed Mom. Her clothes were still in her closet. Her lotions were still in the bathroom. You could still smell her little sachet things when you walked into the bedroom.

But Mom was gone.

I felt like slamming my fist through the motel ceiling above me. I felt like I had bad breath. I felt like I stank. I felt if I didn't sleep soon, I'd explode like a white-hot star, and everything would disappear—Florida, the boat, my brothers, and Dad, everything—sucked into the deep, black hole that was me.

CHAPTER TWO

MY MOM'S NAME was Christine Emily Byron and this is what I can tell you about her. The last time I hugged her, I was exactly as tall as she was. Your own mom always seems so big, and then one day you have this shock of realizing you are as tall as she is. Then you see that after all she is small.

Mom had dark hair that she always kept in a ponytail. She wore jeans, never skirts. She took care of the house and she worked in the garden and she teased Dad, especially when he quoted poetry at us. Like, maybe we'd be taking a walk in the woods by the lake in the fall and Dad would stop and sweep his arms toward the trees and say, "'Margaret, are you grieving over Goldengrove unleaving?'" And Mom would say, "Jim, how many times do I have to tell you—my name is Christine."

When Mom died, everyone wanted to help. Dad's sister flew down. The other professors at the university took over Dad's classes. My friend Andrew even wanted to take me to a game, but I didn't go. I stayed at home with my brothers while Dad sat in the dark and read poems. He'd be quiet for a while and then read us a line. "Listen to this, boys," he would say. "'Do not go gentle into that good night. Rage, rage against the dying of the light.'" Then he would cover his face with his hands. After a while he would say, "Isn't it time for you guys to be in bed?" So we went to bed and we didn't come back downstairs. We didn't want to surprise him. It was too easy to catch him crying.

When it was time to dress for the funeral, he went into his room and shut the door. Usually he helped with our ties, but this time I had to do it for everyone. When we were walking to the car, he stopped and looked at us.

"Did you tie your own ties?" he asked.

"Ben did it," Gerry said.

"He did a good job," Dad said, then rubbed Gerry's head.

"You messed up his hair," I said.

"He didn't," Gerry said.

"Not much," Dylan said quietly.

"I like it this way." Gerry held his hands over his head.

"Be quiet," Dad said. "All of you. Get in the car."

We got in the car, and I sat in the front seat. *Mom's seat,* I thought, and closed my eyes. When we got home, I was so tired I wanted to go straight to bed, but all these people were at our house, standing around talking in low voices and eating sandwiches. I went to the kitchen, and there was Aunt Sue, loading another platter.

"Where's Dad?" I asked her.

"He's upstairs."

"He belongs down here."

"He'll be down soon," she said, and put her arm around my shoulders. She squeezed me a little, then stepped away. "Give him time, Ben. He'll be all right."

I picked up one of the sandwiches. "It's not fair," I said, and squashed the sandwich in my hand.

"Ben! Don't do that." She unrolled my fingers, took out the sandwich, and dropped it in the trash. She handed me a cloth to clean my hand, then picked up the platter of sandwiches and left.

I wiped my hand and turned to lean my forehead against the refrigerator. It was cool and vibrated slightly. It would have been good, I thought, to disappear right then. To disintegrate. Then the refrigerator cycled off. I stood up straight and turned around. Gerry was standing in the kitchen looking at me. He held Blankie bunched up against his mouth. He lowered it a little. "Are you okay, Ben?"

I nodded.

"I'm okay, too," he said.

I sat in a chair and pulled him into my lap. He leaned his head against my shoulder. That close up, I could smell Blankie. It smelled like sleeping and yesterday and all our lives before today.

I picked up a corner and pressed it to my nose.

"It smells good, doesn't it," Gerry said, and I nodded.

CHAPTER THREE

THAT FIRST MORNING in Key West I woke up with Blankie half under my head and Gerry breathing in my face. Dylan was looking out the window. When I sat up, he turned toward me.

"Dad's gone to see the boat and do some shopping at the marina store," he said.

"Great," I said. "What time is it?"

"Lunchtime," he answered.

We called for pizza. When I ate the last piece, I balled up my napkin and tossed it in a perfect arc into the trash can. "Three points," I said. Dylan smoothed his napkin on his thigh. I grabbed it and tossed it in too. "Three points again. The champ rules!"

Nobody said anything.

"What is the name of this boat again?" I asked.

"*Chrysalis,*" Dylan said.

"Does it mean anything?" Gerry asked. He threw his napkin. It fell on the floor.

"It's a scientific term," Dylan said. "It's the cocoon stage of a butterfly or moth."

Gerry picked up his napkin, sat down, and threw again. He missed again.

"Then why don't they just say 'cocoon'?" Gerry asked, and tried his napkin again. Missed. It fell on the bed.

"Sounds like a girl's name," I said. "Should be a perfume or something like that."

Gerry picked up his napkin, threw it again, and missed. "Sounds like Mom's name to me," he said.

"For Pete's sake!" I snatched up the napkin and threw it toward the trash can. "Make the shot, will you!" But I threw too hard. The napkin sailed right over the trash can and fell on the floor.

"Missed," Gerry said.

"Shut up." I lay back on the bed. I closed my eyes.

Wind Racer, I thought. Now that was a good name. Or *Sea Hawk. Wave Dancer* or *Free Time* or *Summer Dream.* All of them were good names. All of them were much better than *Chrysalis.* Even no name at all would be better than that.

The boat we had sailed on the lake at home didn't have a name. We just called it "the boat," and we sailed it every chance we got. Dad even talked about sailing it around the world. When I was little, I believed him. He made up stories about sailing through tsunamis and living off the land in Tahiti. We read *Kon-Tiki* and *Dove* and *Alone Around the World*. Then after Mom was pregnant the last time, he didn't talk about it anymore. I decided he had never really meant it, and I was glad, because I wanted to play baseball and go to summer camp and get a car.

But he had meant it, and he did not forget.

About two months after Mom died, we got home from school one afternoon to see a FOR SALE sign in the yard. "Don't worry," I told Dylan and Gerry. "This house will never sell. Mom always said it was too small."

That night I called for Chinese again and the guy brought all the wrong stuff. I was just starting to make Gerry a peanut butter sandwich when Dad came home.

"I guess you guys saw I listed the house for sale," he said. "I was going to tell you first. I didn't know the sign would go up so fast."

"Why would you want to sell the house?" I asked.

"It's a surprise," he said. "I'll explain over dinner. Sit down."

"I'm making Gerry a sandwich."

"Gerry has to learn to eat what's on the table," Dad said. "When we're on the boat, our diet will be very limited."

We all looked at Dad, but he just kept on serving himself.

"Boat?" I finally asked.

"That's the surprise," he said.

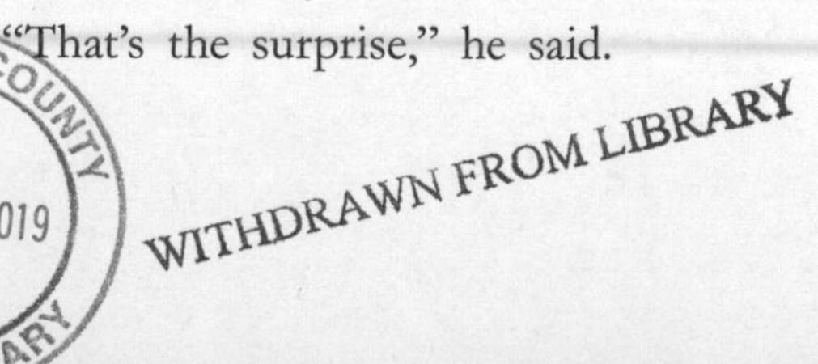